RED TIDE

BOOKS IN THE STELLAR GUILD SERIES

Tau Ceti by Kevin J. Anderson & Steven Savile

Reboots by Mercedes Lackey & Cody Martin

On The Train by Harry & Rachel Turtledove

When the Blue Shift Comes by Robert Silverberg
& Alvaro Zinos-Amaro

New Under the Sun by Nancy Kress
& Therese Pieczynski

The Aethers of Mars by Eric Flint
& Charles E. Gannon

WWW.STELLARGUILD.COM

RED TIDE

LARRY NIVEN

ADDITIONAL WORKS BY

BRAD R. TORGERSEN

AND

MATTHEW J. HARRINGTON

THE STELLAR GUILD SERIES
TEAM-UPS WITH BESTSELLING AUTHORS

MIKE RESNICK
SERIES EDITOR

an imprint of

Rockville, Maryland

Series edited by Mike Resnick.

ISBN: 978-1-61242-132-2

www.PhoenixPick.com
Great Science Fiction & Fantasy
Free Ebook every month

Published by Phoenix Pick
an imprint of Arc Manor
P. O. Box 10339
Rockville, MD 20849-0339
www.ArcManor.com

CONTENTS

A GREETING FROM THE SERIES EDITOR

WELCOME TO THE STELLAR GUILD. In every book we've combined a new novella by an established star with a novelette or novella—a prequel, sequel, or companion piece—by a protégé of the star's own choosing. Our first few books featured Kevin J. Anderson, Mercedes Lackey, Robert Silverberg, Harry Turtledove, Nancy Kress, and Eric Flint—and the very first book in the series, *Tau Ceti*, by Kevin and his protégé, Steven Savile, won the Lifeboat To The Stars Award.

This time we're doing something just a little different. Our star, Larry Niven, has been one of the brightest in the field of science fiction for about half a century now—and for this book he has *two* protégés, Matthew J. Harrington and Brad R. Torgersen. While Larry and Gregory Benford (the science columnist for our *Galaxy's Edge* magazine) were busy collaborating on the bestselling *Bowl of Heaven*, he suggested that Matthew and Brad study his novella "Flash Crowd" for the venue, the time and place and conditions, that he wanted them to write about. When they had each completed their novelettes and Larry had finished *Bowl of Heaven*, he went to work expanding "Flash Crowd," which is now "Red Tide," and then as a bonus he wrote a new story, "Dial at Random," which is just a few words shy of novelette length itself.

   We think it's a unique team-up, and we hope you'll like it as much as we do.

Mike Resnick

RED TIDE

A Word From Larry Niven

THIS BOOK TAUGHT ME a writer's lesson.

In 1973 I had promised Robert Silverberg a story about teleportation. My notion was that my form of teleportation would obey all the conservation laws of high school physics. When inspiration didn't come, I used a writer's trick: I made two lists.

First, I listed everything I would expect to happen if teleport booths became commercial. What happens to airports, to traffic, newspapers, etc. Second, who gets hurt? (Following one of Theodore Sturgeon's rules. He who gets hurt is your main character.) I wrote Bob a story from those lists. With a new universe to play with, I wrote four more stories, crime stories.

N-Space is a collection Tor published in 1990. For that book Robert Gleason collected quotes about me from a variety of sources. David Brin accused me of stealing his ideas before he'd thought of them: "If you think that the territory of notions is limited, then the hard SF writer is like a wildcat miner drilling into resources that are shrinking ... If their reasoning is true—and I don't think it is—one of the reasons is that you have writers like Larry Niven out there mining out whole veins and leaving nothing left for the rest of us to explore." I was pleased and flattered and grateful to David for doing this, and I never considered that there might be anything in it. I don't believe ideas are limited either.

So it's late 2012, and here comes Mike Resnick with a suggestion. Let's get an established writer (me) together with a younger writer, and we'll each write a new story set in the same fictional universe! This notion isn't a crapshoot: Mike has been trying it and it works. "Great!" I said. "We'll use the Flash Crowd universe. It's forty years old and hasn't hardly been touched. And I've got a novice in mind," and I offered Matthew Harrington. He'd written several dynamite stories for the Man-Kzin War volumes, and we'd done a novel too (*The Goliath Stone*). Mike had a writer in mind too, and that was Brad Torgersen. I didn't know Brad as well, but heyyy. We agreed to put two younger writers in this volume, and I'd shorten my novella. Hah! Less work.

So I sat down to write. I made some notes, and got stuck. David Brin had used the word "rapacious," and he was right. Sonofabitch. Forty years ago, a younger Larry Niven had moved into the territory of rationalized teleportation and stripped it of every implication, leaving nothing for me.

Well, not quite. I was stuck for three or four months. But I remembered an old idea, never touched, and I wrote "Dial at Random." Meanwhile Brad suggested that without the rules laid out in "Flash Crowd" our readers could be left hopelessly confused. I agreed, and told Mike. In the end, and with Brad's help, I rewrote and expanded "Flash Crowd" into "Red Tide." Start reading there.

Larry Niven

BOOK ONE: RED TIDE

LARRY NIVEN

PROLOGUE

BARRY JEROME JANSEN WAS TWELVE years old when he witnessed the last recorded car-on-car traffic accident in the state of California.

Standing outside an ice cream shop, Barry was spectating an impromptu parade of vintage automobiles, all being driven along the historic Highway 1. The cars were headed north, to a classic auto convention in San Francisco. Drivers smiled at the pedestrians who came out to gawk. Convertible tops were down. Engines mutually rumbled—the kind of sound that was odd in Barry's ears, but which seemed to elicit a gleam of pleasant reverie from Barry's father's eyes. Before quickly being replaced by a too-familiar, taciturn glare.

On that late Sunday morning, Barry paid his father no mind. Barry was rapt. Watching the cars roll past was a little like watching a fleet of stagecoaches trundle by: pieces of famous technology, each passing into history. Overall, the automobile was an amazing machine. The useful lifespan of which had lasted roughly about as long as the typewriter. Not bad. Cars had been essential to the genesis of the 21st century. But now their day was over.

Barry felt an instinct to salute.

He got a shock when a polished, purple El Camino nosed into the back of a gleaming, steel-grey Jaguar.

It was a quick sound: *scrunch!*

Almost immediately, Barry and his father were politely shouldered out of the way by a young woman with a camera in her hand.

She had on a headset and was talking quietly into the microphone boom that delicately traced along one cheek, down toward her thin-lipped mouth. She was also freckled and wearing shorts with a tank top. Perhaps all of nineteen years old?

Barry instantly assumed she was a tourist.

But ... no.

She held herself with entirely too much poise. And seemed to be conversing as if in a detached manner.

A small crowd gathered as the drivers each exited their cars, surveyed the damage, then began shaking their heads.

And almost as fast, a pair of uniformed California Highway Patrol officers appeared. The two women—still wearing characteristic mirror-lensed aviator sunglasses—had come without a car of their own.

And while they began to discuss the details of the wreck with the owners—one cop directing traffic around the accident, while the other cop typed up a ticket on her digital pad—Barry merely stared at the girl with the camera. She was slowly scanning her device back and forth, all the way around the scene. And though Barry couldn't hear precisely what she was saying, he suspected that what she was saying was important.

And he was right.

Later that evening when Barry and his father returned home, there on the news was the evidence: high-resolution footage of the scene of the accident, including the accident itself. No injuries reported, thankfully. Just some bruised feelings between hobbyists who'd now be spending even more money to repair and revitalize their expensive collectible contraptions.

As Barry watched the news and listened to the slow, confident words of the young woman speaking over the footage, he felt an electric tickle at the back of his brain. The woman wasn't much older than him, yet she was right there, detailing events. Making history.

For an instant, Barry and his father flashed into view. Both of them had their eyes focused on the wreck.

"The lady we saw today," Barry asked, "the one with the camera—is she a reporter?"

Eric Jansen was seated in his use-worn easy chair in the family's smallish living room. Most nights he kept to his e-reader, giving the TV no thought.

Realizing he'd been asked a question, Barry's father looked up: eyes tired.

"They don't call them reporters anymore, but yes. We were just dumb-fool fortunate enough to be standing there when that fender bender happened. It seems silly now, that this kind of thing makes the evening news. A few years ago nobody cared about a wreck unless it was a multi-car pileup on the Interstate."

Barry's father sighed, and went back to his e-reader.

But Barry had been struck dumb.

The idea, of capturing that moment … on the scene, in the instant, recording it all for the masses … a kind of fame, yes. But a kind of power, too!

Barry looked around at the modest, anonymously decorated house he'd lived in ever since he was a toddler, and swore to himself that he'd become just like the woman with the camera.

"In the old days we used to call you cub reporters," said the collection desk controller for the *Golden State Bulletin-Gazette*. She was past middle-aged, with a head full of cornrows which had just begun to turn silver at the roots. Her brown skin was nicely complexioned, and her eyes were sharp: the kind of eyes that told you in one glance they'd seen it all before.

Barry was standing with five other teenagers just behind the collection desk proper, where the controller—Sharlaqueen—was giving them their orientation. Theirs was not a paid gig, of course. This was strictly intern work. The kind of thing intended to teach and season raw novices. Of which Barry was one in a long line to have passed through Sharlaqueen's hands.

"Now we're newstapers?" said the teen to Barry's left, a tallish Chinese fellow who seemed so full of energy he couldn't keep still.

"Not yet," Sharlaqueen said. "Do any of you know what the difference is, between a proper *newstaper*—and some idiot with a digital phone camera?"

The six youths slowly shook their heads.

"It's the ability to keep cool under fire," Sharlaqueen said. "This is not a crazy home movies production we run at the *Bulletin-Gazette*—pushing out shit videos of your friends doing faceplants off their skateboards. The *Golden State Bulletin-Gazette* is a serious news source, and gets fifteen *million* unique hits per day. Our advertisers are depending on us to keep our content professional. Got it?"

Barry nodded dumbly. He was sure he didn't get it. Yet. But he did remember the woman he'd seen at the car wreck, when he was younger. She'd watched and narrated the whole thing like she had ice in her veins. No excited exclamations, nor any herky-jerky movements. Smooth as silk. That's what Barry wanted to be, too.

He still wondered how much that woman had made for her footage. Which eventually broadcast all over California, and nationally too—once the newswires picked it up as a color piece.

Barry had heard rumors that such a spot—going viral—could net a newstaper *tens of thousands* of dollars. Riches beyond imagination for a young man Barry's age. All he needed was experience. A track record to hang his hat on, and peddle either to the permanent hiring office at the *Bulletin-Gazette* or elsewhere.

Sharlaqueen was right. Any fool could use a digital device to snap footage. It took a steady hand and a steady mind to be a pro.

Barry was itching to go, despite his father's reluctant approval.

Anything to get out of the damned house …

"This is the nerve center," Sharlaqueen said, motioning her arm across her desk. "I keep tabs on every newstaper on the *Bulletin-Gazette*'s books. Any time anyone's got something for me to look at, the alert comes here. Where I evaluate the material—either live or recorded—and determine whether or not to push it to the team upstairs."

"So you control what's news?" asked a girl to the other side of the Chinese boy. She was overly short, and somewhat plump, but with an inquisitive bearing.

"I suppose you could say I am a first-level filter," Sharlaqueen said. "And I've been doing this job for longer than any of you children have been alive. So if you want to get in good with the *Bulletin-Gazette*, you'd better pay attention to the directions I'll be giving you. Send me too much bullshit, and I'll order your internship scrubbed. I don't have time to waste with amateurs. From this point forward you all should start thinking and acting like newspeople. Understood?"

A short chorus of *yes-ma'am*s.

They were each given an expensive set of gear: a stabilized camera, with microphone, and a headpiece. The total cost of which was made quite plain, due to the fact that if any of them lost or damaged the equipment, it would be assessed against them as a credit debt.

When Barry had the temerity to ask how the *Golden State Bulletin-Gazette* could afford to trust teenagers with such pricey electronics, Sharlaqueen informed them that it was a calculated risk. One that usually made the company more money than it lost, in the form of quality newstapers who developed into competent deliverers of bona fide content. Which kept the readership and viewership happy, and thus the advertising dollars remained consistent.

His first day on the job, Barry spent his time fumbling around the *Bulletin-Gazette* offices. Under the watchful eye of one of the veteran special interest newstapers who'd come in at Sharlaqueen's request. To train the new batch of interns on how to use the stabilized camera system to full effect, how to move slowly and talk without too much *umm* and *errrr*, as well as how to look for potentially newsworthy footage.

"You won't know it until it happens," he finally said.

The man's name was Horace Lamarquez—a name Barry recognized from the news. Horace had done a lot of local and even a few national pieces. Not precisely a famous newstaper, Horace nevertheless had the chops to know what he was talking about. Barry listened intently, and raised his hand to ask questions.

Which he did quite often.

"Yes, Barry?" Horace said.

"If we won't know it until it happens, what's the point in going out to try to look for it?"

"It's like this," Horace said, fingering the moustache under his nose. "A good newstaper never stands still. She gets out into the city, or into the world, and she learns to have an instinct for what *might* happen, and where. Of course, some of the best newstaper footage in recent memory is the kind no person could possibly plan for. Remember the four-alarm fire last week? One of my friends was standing in line at a store in the very shopping mall where the fire happened. He had the good sense to turn his camera on. That footage went national. My friend's now going to take a vacation in the Bahamas."

The teenagers chuckled.

But Barry was suddenly seeing dollar signs.

The right newstaper, at the right place, at the right time …

Luck would favor the intrepid, or so Barry hoped.

He started his adventure the next day.

On the street, it wasn't nearly as easy as Barry had imagined it would be. And some of the first clips he sent back to Sharlaqueen got bounced with some rather unflattering commentary. Her critiques were pointed. Almost hurtful. But Barry tried to take it in stride. He'd come to the internship believing that newstaping was his future. A way out of his father's house. A path to, if not fame per se, at least a little bit of fortune. And a chance to be part of things larger than any single person. Momentous, even?

After the first day of fruitless effort, and then the second, and then the third, Barry caught himself wistfully wishing for a disaster. Like the mall fire Horace had mentioned. Mayhem! Explosions! Maybe a tsunami? An earthquake ought to provide work for a thousand newstapers, full-time.

Then Barry quietly quashed these thoughts, and berated himself for ever thinking them in the first place.

Being on the scene for something bad, and actively *hoping* for something bad, were two entirely different things. Barry wasn't quite comfortable with himself for having gone down that road. What did it say about his character?

After a fourth day spent aimlessly wandering the city— looking for news that didn't happen—Barry reluctantly discussed his feelings with Horace.

"Jerryberry," Horace said, using the nickname that Sharlaqueen had hung on Barry the morning of day two, "we've all experienced the desire: to be in the midst of something so cataclysmic and overwhelming, that every second of footage is historic. The kind of stuff they'll put on the national or world news and run for days or weeks. Do you know what the *Hindenburg* was?"

"No," Barry admitted.

"Long time ago, before even I was born—so you know it's been a while—they used to make blimps filled with hydrogen, instead of helium. Airships, they were called. Anyway, the *Hindenburg* was this great big airship that used to take people across the Atlantic ocean. Then one day as she was pulling into New Jersey, the *Hindenburg* burst into flames. And there were cameras and a man with a microphone there to report it. Herbert Morrison. His voice recording of the event went on to become world-famous, even long after he died."

"Whoa," Barry said, his eyes gone wide.

"Now," Horace said, putting a hand on Barry's shoulder, "the chances of you or I ever standing in Herbert Morrison's shoes are remote. You can wish for such a thing, but it's more probable that you won't get to have a Herbert Morrison moment. And that's OK. Not every clip need be about astounding disasters or tragedies. You should think outside the box a little. Look for good news. Or interesting events that spring up. Maybe even interesting people connected to interesting events? In my entire career I've never been there for a *Hindenburg*-style whopper. But I've gotten very good at digging for the stories-beneath-the-story, if you catch my drift?"

Barry just nodded.

And went back out on the street for a fifth day.

The city seemed as devoid of actual news as ever.

Then Barry strolled past the construction site on I-5.

The decommissioning of the freeways wasn't news anymore. Traffic had tapered down to the point that politicians could not justify the tax dollars to keep them up, so the onramps were barricaded and the all-but-empty freeways became an obsolete curiosity. Reminders of life in the previous century. Remanded to local state and municipal control.

Even the military didn't see a need for them anymore— and it had been the military which had caused freeways to come into being in the wake of World War Two.

In California, many of the freeways sat utterly derelict.

But here and there, people were putting them to good use.

A brick-and-mortar superstore was being put up right in the middle of a twelve-lane section of the mighty mid-town Interstate. Three stories tall. With skybridges. Acres of eventual shopping space. Barry found himself fascinated by the surreal sight of men and heavy equipment moving huge steel beams into place, then bolting them directly down to the use-worn surface of the freeway's concrete.

Some of the huge crane trucks had to weigh many tons.

Hmmmm …

Barry waited until one of the crane operators took a break.

In the meantime he got several minutes of interesting footage of the crane doing its work.

When the crane stopped moving and the door on the crane's cab popped open, Barry chased up to the fence surrounding the construction lot and waved for the crane operator's attention—newstaper camera held high.

The crane operator sauntered over.

"Hiya, kid," the man said, pulling off his hardhat and wiping his shining scalp with a handkerchief. "Helluva day to be parked on the concrete."

"Sure is," Barry said, feeling his own shirt grow damp at the waist and around the pits of his arms. "Would you mind if I asked you a few questions about this project? It's for the *Golden State Bulletin-Gazette*."

"Sure," the operator said, smiling.

"Can I come inside the fence?" Barry asked.

"Better if I come outside of it."

Which the man did.

Together, Barry and the operator—who identified himself as John Griggs—took a seat under one of the many tents surrounding the work site. Huge buckets of ice water and chilled, fruity electrolyte drink were perched on picnic tables, and Barry and John each filled themselves a foam cup before sitting on a bench and having a conversation.

"How did the crane get here?" Barry asked.

"Beg pardon?"

"If the freeways are closed, how did the crane get to the work site?"

"Well ... we drove it, naturally. Special permit from the city."

"And what happens when the freeway has been used up for other stores, or parks, or anything else people might want to lay down over the top of the concrete? How will you be getting the cranes where they need to be?"

John thought about it, rubbing his black moustache.

"I suppose we'd have to fly it in."

"By helicopter?"

"It'd be the only way."

"Are there helicopters big enough to lift a crane truck like yours?"

"The Army or Forest Service might have some, I think. Huge birds. When I was a kid they were called Aircranes. With gargantuan rotors that flexed upward at the tips when they were lifting."

"A crane to lift a *crane*?"

"Yuh," John said, smiling and chuckling, then taking a long drink. "If you want, I can maybe get you a day permit on the site. Show you how the controls to my machine work."

Barry beamed.

"Could you?"

"Sure. The foreman might love the publicity, having a junior newstaper showing off the company logo all nice and big on the side of the truck. Let's go to the trailer and get you authorized."

They walked to a double-wide unit chocked up on cinder blocks.

Inside, several in-window air conditioners chugged noisily.

"What's your name, kid," the middle-aged woman at the desk said as she scrawled Barry's temporary credentials on an orange lanyard.

"Jerryberry," he blurted.

"What?" the woman asked.

"Sorry," Barry said, ashamed to admit that the nickname had stuck, even in his mind. "Barry Jerome Jansen."

"I think I liked it better the first time," she said, shaking her head and chewing her gum.

She wrote JERRY BERRY in all caps, using a permanent marker.

The crane operator smiled at Barry, then got official permission from the foreman, and took Barry over to climb up into the cab.

Barry's was the first piece from any of his intern peers to actually make it through Sharlaqueen's jaundiced sieve. And that of the people upstairs. And even onto the wider state media scan.

Because it wasn't just the crane that proved interesting.

The helicopter portion was interesting too. Barry went directly to a company that leased helicopters for construction airlift, and managed to spend time in the cockpit with one of the pilots. He even got a short ride while the pilot and a co-pilot took one of the huge machines up for a maintenance hop across town.

Barry digitally recorded and talked his way through the whole thing.

Properly edited, the piece made for a nice bit of variety news.

And it got Barry a bonus, which he'd not been expecting.

"It's not often they give these out to kids," Sharlaqueen said when she slipped Barry the envelope. "But the people upstairs were so pleased with the performance of your story, they let it be known that you deserved at least some portion of the profit."

Barry opened the envelope.

It was more money than he'd ever held in one hand in his entire life.

Sharlaqueen smiled.

"Keep it up, Jerryberry. Most kids who come through my door looking to make it as a newstaper, wash out within two weeks. On account of boredom. But you? You seem to be the kind of person who just might make a go of it. Show me a few more pieces like this one, and you won't have any trouble coming on full-time."

"Yes ma'am," Barry said, grinning from ear to ear.

He left work that day, practically at a run. He couldn't wait to show the check to his father.

"It'll take more than five hundred bucks to pay rent in this city," Eric Jansen groused over the dinner table.

Barry's mother had been momentarily excited for Barry when he'd rushed in the door, envelope in hand. But that excitement had been summarily silenced by Eric Jansen's un-impressed reception.

"It's just a start, dad," Barry said, his tone revealing his impatience with his father's criticism.

Eric just stared at his son: a bushy, fatherly eyebrow raised.

"Sorry, sir," Barry muttered.

"And how many hours did it take you to earn this?" Eric asked.

"Six, maybe seven?"

"Try forty," Eric said. "Because it took you all week to come up with *one* good piece. And then the company took the lion's share of your earnings. Hell, son, you might as well set up your own damned web site and go into business solo."

"I won't get any market traction that way," Barry said. "The only solo newstapers making money are the ones who started off with the big sites, and gained enough of an individual following to split off. I have to start small. Work my way up."

"It's his first paycheck, Eric," Barry's mother mildly scolded her husband. "The least we can do is be thankful that he's out trying to earn money. Unlike some of our friends' kids. You know the Fredricks' boy is already twenty five and he's *still* not worked a day in his life? Your son will be sixteen next year, and he's earning *now*."

Barry beamed.

Eric Jansen remained unconvinced. His fingers drummed his thigh.

"So how long before you make *real* money?"

"Not long," Barry said, half hoping it was true. "My boss says if I turn in a couple more solid pieces like the one I did today, they'll take me on permanently. I get a quarterly stipend, plus better equipment. I can use the money to go to journalism school. Get an actual degree. When I graduate, I can take a shot at one of the major networks."

"That's a long ways in the future," Eric said. "And what guarantee will you have that you'll keep getting lucky? Finding news worth their time and dollars? Seems to me this boss of yours has her finger on the pulse of whether you'll starve on any given week. I don't like it."

"You don't have to like it!" Barry exploded, his adolescent temper having reached its end. He'd known the argument was coming. He'd been dreading it ever since he officially approached the *Bulletin-Gazette*. But now that the argument was in full swing, Barry found he had absolutely no appetite for it. None. Why did dad always have to be this way?

Eric Jansen slapped his hand commandingly on the kitchen table.

"Now look," he said, leaning in to stare directly into Barry's hotly glaring eyes, "as long as you're under this roof I demand some basic respect. You're not a man yet, you hear me? Just because you had a stroke of luck and got a little money in your pocket, you think you're ready to go out and swing a bat with the big boys? Do you? Well you're not. Believe me. I know what it's like to fall on my face, son. It can happen at any time, anywhere."

"It's better to try, and fail, than to not try at all," Barry said with a thick voice as he swallowed back the tears.

Eric Jansen simply kept staring into his son's now-red eyes.

Then Barry's father's shoulders drooped, and he muttered a few choice four letter words, then stood up and plodded back through the kitchen door to where his use-worn easy chair awaited him.

Eric's mother reached across the table and put her hand on one of Barry's. He sniffed twice, finally allowing a few drops to leak down his face.

"Don't be too mad at him," Barry's mother said. "It's not been easy. Your father didn't have to work until much later in his life than you're having to work now. He just doesn't want to see you get disappointed the way he got disappointed."

"Dad never had a dream, Mom," Barry said. "I do."

"I know that, dear," she said, "and I think it's wonderful to see you trying so hard. But the summer won't last forever. And you still have school to worry about in September.

Are you going to be running around all evening after class, chasing stories? When you should be doing homework?"

"I don't know," Barry admitted.

"Well, we'll cross that bridge when we come to it," she finally said, offering her son a cautious smile.

It was a couple of weeks before Barry turned in anything else worthy of Sharlaqueen's approval. And then, a few more weeks again. When school came, Barry had to limit his activities to weekends, but it was worth it to him to keep bringing in the occasional bonus check, just to brandish it in his father's sour face.

Months rolled onward.

By the time Jerryberry was sixteen, he'd been brought on part-time.

At eighteen, he forgot all about journalism school and went full-time.

Newstaping became his obsession. He traveled extensively from San Diego in the south to Sacramento in the north. He sent in countless variety pieces, bits of political reporting, follow-up stories connected to bigger news that had already passed from public attention, and then he struck gold. He got on the national scene with an extensive in-progress report on a bank robbery involving armed and armored gunmen lugging semiautomatic rifles and lobbing smoke grenades.

That spectacular piece got Jerryberry noticed in a big way.

The very next morning, he had the offer he'd been waiting for. Sitting in his e-mail box.

Sharlaqueen's expression was knowing when Jerryberry came through her door that afternoon.

"They want you," was all she said.

"Yes," Jerryberry admitted, somewhat sheepishly.

"I knew it," she said. "I've known it for a long time. The good ones always get taken. Newstaping is a lot like baseball. Talent rises. And you've got talent. It took a bit of honing, which I'll happily take credit for. But like I told Horace when you started sending me the footage from the robbery yesterday, this was going to be your ticket up. Congratulations."

"Thanks, Shar, I really appreciate it. Look, ummm, I don't exactly want to have to say that I quit. I like you and I like the *Bulletin-Gazette*. Any chance we could set up some kind of special arrangement?"

"Have you seen your new contract with the big network?" she asked.

"No, just the offer. It's a nice one. I can't turn it down."

"I know you can't. And I wouldn't want you to. Look, unless they're crazy, your contract won't allow you to freelance for any other company. They'll claim every second of everything you newstape from now until the contract expires. Just remember who taught you everything you know, okay? And if things get tight and you need to fall back, the *Golden State Bulletin-Gazette*'s doors are always open."

"Thanks, Shar," Jerryberry said.

He put out his hand as she stood up from behind her desk and walked around to where he was standing.

Grabbing his hand, she pulled him into a bear hug.

"Go get 'em," Sharlaqueen said in his ear.

"I hope I don't let you down," Jerryberry responded, feeling a lump in his throat.

-]-

FROM EDGE TO EDGE and for all of its length, from Central Los Angeles through Beverly Hills and West Los Angeles and Santa Monica to the sea, Wilshire Boulevard was a walkway.

Once there had been white lines on concrete, and raised curbs to stop the people from interfering with the cars. Now the lines were gone, and much of the concrete was covered with soil and grass. There were even a few trees. Concrete strips had been left for bicycles, and wider places for helicopters carrying cargo too big for the displacement booths.

Wilshire was wide for a walkway. People seemed to hug the edges, even those on bikes and motor skates. A boulevard built for cars was too big for mere people.

Outlines of the street still showed through. Ridges in the grass marked where curbs had been, with breaks where there had been driveways. Some stretches in Westwood had a concrete center divider. The closed freeway ramps were unchanged and unused. Someday the city would do something about them.

Jerryberry Jansen lived in what had been a seaside motel halfway between Bakersfield and San Francisco. On long-ago summer nights the Shady Rest had been packed with transients at ten dollars a head. Now it made a dandy apartment house, with swimming pool and everything, including a displacement booth outside the manager's office.

There was a girl in the booth when Jerryberry left his apartment. He glimpsed long, wavy brown hair and the shape of her back in the instant before she disappeared. Janice Wolfe. Too bad she hadn't waited ... but she hadn't even seen him.

Nobody was ever around the booths long enough to say hello to. You could meet someone by hovering outside the booths, but what would they think?

Meeting people was for the clubs.

A displacement booth was a glass cylinder with a rounded top. The machinery that made the magic was invisible, buried beneath the booth. Coin slots and a telephone dial were set into the glass at sternum level.

Jerryberry inserted his C.B.A. credit card below the coin slot. He dialed by punching numbered buttons. Withdrawing the credit card closed a circuit. An eye blink later he was in an office in the Central Broadcasting Association building in downtown Los Angeles.

The office was big and empty. Only once in an aeon was all that empty space ever used, though several score of newstapers saw it for a few seconds each day. One wall was lined with displacement booths. A curved desk down at the end was occupied by Jerryberry's network boss.

Unlike Sharlaqueen, George Bailey was fat from too much sitting. His skin was darkly tanned by the Nevada sun. He commuted to work every morning via the long-distance booths at Los Angeles International. Today he waved at Jerryberry without speaking. Routine, then. Jerryberry chose one of several C.B.A.-issue cameras and slung the padded strap over his shoulder. He studied several lists of numbers posted over the table before picking one.

He turned and moved to avoid three more newstapers stepping out of booths. They nodded; he nodded; they passed. As he reached for a booth door, a woman flicked in in front of him. Rush hour. He smiled at her and stepped over to the next booth, consulted the list, dialed, and was gone.

He had not spoken to anyone that morning.

The east end of Wilshire Boulevard was a most ordinary T-intersection between high, blocky buildings. Jerryberry looked around even as he was dialing. Nothing newsworthy? No. He was two blocks away and dialing.

He punched the numbered buttons with a ballpoint pen when he remembered. Nonetheless, his index finger was calloused. It had been a long time since he'd used buses to get around. The city didn't operate them anymore.

The streets of the inner city were empty, this early. In a minute or so Jerryberry was in sight of the vacant freeway. He stepped out of the booth to watch trucks and bulldozers covering this part of the Pasadena-Harbor Freeway with topsoil. *Old machines find new use*—but others were covering the event. He moved on.

The booths were all identical. He might have been in a full-vision theater, watching scenes flick around him. He was used to the way things jerked about. He flicked west on Wilshire, waiting for something to happen.

It was a cheap, effective way to gather news. A technique Jerryberry had picked up shortly after being hired on at C.B.A. At a dollar per jump per man, C.B.A. could afford to support scores of wandering newstapers in addition to their regular investigative staff.

Instead of a quarterly stipend, Jerryberry now earned a modest monthly salary, plus a bonus for each news item that got George Bailey's stamp of approval. These days, the bonuses had more zeroes compared to the ones the *Golden State Bulletin-Gazette* had given out. Especially for major breaking stories guaranteed to generate huge traffic on C.B.A.'s livestream channels, not to mention TV viewership.

Jerryberry Jansen knew every foot of Wilshire. At twenty-four he was old enough to remember cars and trucks and traffic lights. When the city changed, it was the streets that had changed most.

He watched Wilshire change as he dialed.

At the old hat-shaped Brown Derby they were converting the parking lot into a miniature golf course. About time they did something with all that wasted space. He queried Bailey, but Bailey wasn't interested.

The Miracle Mile was a landscaped section. Suddenly there were people: throngs of shoppers, so thick that many preferred to walk a block instead of waiting for a booth. They seemed stratified, with the older people hugging the curbs and the teens taking the middle of the street. Jerryberry had noticed it before. As a child he'd been trained to cross only in the crosswalks, with the light. Sometimes his training came back, and he found himself looking both ways before he could step out from the curb.

He moved on, west, following the list of numbers that was his beat.

The mall had been a walkway when displacement booths were no more than a theorem in quantum mechanics. Dips in the walk showed where streets had crossed, but the Santa Monica Mall had always been a sanctuary for pedestrians and window-shoppers. Here were several blocks of shops and restaurants and theaters, low buildings that did not block the sky.

Displacement booths were thick here. People swarmed constantly around and in and out of them. Some travelers carried fold-up bicycles. Many wore change purses. From noon onward there was always the tension of too many people trying to use the same space for the same purpose.

The argument started outside a department store. At the time one could see only that the police officer was being firm and the woman—middle-aged, big, and brawny—was screaming at the top of her lungs. A crowd grew, not because anyone gave a damn but because the two were blocking the walkway. People had to stream around them.

Some of them stopped to see what was happening. Many later remembered hearing the policeman repeating, "Madam, I place you under arrest on suspicion of shoplifting. Anything you say—" in a voice that simply did not carry. If the officer had used his shockstick then, nothing more would have happened. Maybe. Then again, he might have been mobbed. Already the crowd blocked the entire mall, and too many of them were shouting—genial or sarcastic suggestions, random insults, and a thousand variations of "Get out of my way!" and "I can't, you idiot!"—for any to be heard at all.

At 12:55 P.M. Jerryberry Jansen flicked in and looked quickly about him while his hands were reinserting his credit card. His eyes registered the ancient shops at the end of the mall and lingered a moment on the entrance to Romanoff's. Anyone newsworthy; sometimes they came, the big names, for the cuisine or the publicity. No? Jerryberry passed on, jumped to the crowd in front of the department store two blocks down.

There were booths nearer, but he didn't know the numbers offhand. Jerryberry picked up his card and stepped out of the booth. He signaled the studio but didn't bother to report. Circumstantial details he could give later. But he turned on his camera, and the event was now ... real.

He jogged the two blocks. Whatever was happening might end without him.

A young, bemused face turned at Jerryberry's hail. "Excuse me, sir. Can you tell me how this started?"

"Nope. Sorry. I just got here," said the young man, and he strolled off—he would be edited from the digital recording in the camera's memory.

But other heads were turning, noticing the arrival of:

Jerryberry—a lean fellow with an open, curious, friendly face, topped by red-blond hair, curly as cotton; a tiny wireless phone combo piece in one ear, a coin purse at his belt.

In Jerryberry's hands—a superlight gyrostabilized digital camera equipped with a directional condenser microphone on a small boom.

Official newstaper, C.B.A.

Jerryberry still relished the title.

One pair of eyes turned toward the camera for an instant too long.

The woman swung her purse.

The policeman's arm came up too late to block the purse, which bounced solidly off his head. Something heavy in that purse.

The policeman dropped.

Things happened very fast.

Jerryberry talked rapidly to himself while he panned the camera. Occasional questions in his earpiece did not interrupt the flow of his report, though they guided it. The gyrostabilized camera felt like a living thing in his hands. It followed the woman with the heavy purse as she pushed her way through the crowd, shot Jerryberry a venomous look, and ran for a displacement booth. It watched someone break a jeweler's window, snatch up a handful of random jewelry, and run. The directional mic picked up the scream of an alarm.

The police officer was still down.

Jerryberry went to help. It occurred to him that of those present, the policeman was most likely to know what had been going on. The voice in his earpiece told him that others were on their way, even as his eye found them leaving the booths: faces he knew on men carrying cameras like his own. He knelt beside the policeman.

"Officer, can you tell me what happened?"

The uniformed man looked up with hurt, bewildered eyes. He said something that the directional mic picked up, but Jerryberry's ears lost it in the crowd noise. He heard it later on the news. "Where's my hat?"

Jerryberry repeated, "What happened here?" while a dozen C.B.A. men around him were interviewing the crowd, and police were pouring out of the displacement booths. The flow of uniforms looked like far more than they were. They had to use their shock-sticks to get through the crowd.

Some of the spectators-shoppers-strollers had decided to leave. A wise decision, but impractical. The nearest booths could not be used at all. They held passengers cased in glass, each trying to get his door open against the press of the mob. Every few seconds one would give up and flick out, and another trapped passenger would be pushing at the door.

For blocks around, there was no way to get into a displacement booth. As fast as anyone left a booth, someone else would flick in. Most were nondescript citizens who came to gape. A few carried big cardboard rectangles carelessly printed in fluorescent colors, often with the paint still wet. A different few, nondescript otherwise, had rocks in their pockets.

For Jerryberry, kneeling above the felled policeman and trying to get audible sense out of him, it all seemed to explode. He looked up, and it was a riot.

"It's a riot," he said, awed. The directional mic picked it up.

Jerryberry felt his heart begin to pound, just as it had during the bank robbery many years before.

The crowd surged, and Jerryberry was moving. He looked back, trying to see if the policeman had gained his feet. If he hadn't, he could be hurt … but the crowd surged away. In this mob there was no conservation of matter; there were sources and sinks in it, and today all the sinks were sources. The flow had to go somewhere.

A young woman pushed herself close to Jerryberry. Her eyes were wide; her hair was wild. A kind of rage, a kind of joy, made her face a battlefield. "Legalize direct-current stimulus!" she screamed at him. She lunged and caught the snout of Jerryberry's camera and mic and pulled it around to face her. "Legalize wireheading!"

Jerryberry wrenched the camera free. He turned it toward the department store's big display window. The glass was gone. Men crawled in the display window, looting. Jerryberry held the camera high, taking pictures of them over the bobbing heads. He had the scene for a moment—and then three signs shot up in front of the camera. One said "TANSTAAFL." and one bore a mushroom cloud and the words "POWER CORRUPTS!" and Jerryberry never read the third because the crowd surged again and he had to scramble to keep his feet. There were men and women and children being trampled here. He could be one of them.

How had it happened? He'd seen it all, but he didn't understand.

He tried to keep the camera over his head. He got a big, brawny, hairy type carrying a stack of flatscreen LCD televisions under his arm: half a dozen twenty-inch sets, each almost an inch thick. The thief saw the camera facing him and the solemn face beneath, and he roared and lunged toward Jerryberry.

Jerryberry abruptly realized that there were people here who would not want to be photographed. The big man had dropped his loot and was plowing toward Jerryberry with murder on his face. Jerryberry had to drop his camera to get away. When he looked back, the big man was smashing the digital camera and gyrostabilizer against a lamp post.

Idiot. The scene was permanent now, broadcast back to the servers in the C.B.A. buildings in Los Angeles and in Denver.

The riot splashed outward. Jerryberry perforce went with it. He concentrated on keeping his feet.

-2-

THE EXPLOSIVE GROWTH of the mall riot took enforcement agencies by surprise. Police managed to hold the perimeter and were letting people through the lines, but necessarily in small numbers.

The screen showed people being filtered through a police blockade, one at a time. They looked tired, stunned. One had two pockets full of stolen wristwatches. He did not protest when they confiscated the watches and led him away. A blank-eyed girl maintained a death grip on a rough wooden stick glued to a cardboard rectangle. The cardboard was crumpled and torn, the Day-Glo colors smeared.

Meanwhile all displacement booths in the area had been shut down from the outside. The enclosed area included fourteen city blocks. Viewers were warned away from the following areas, et cetera.

Top-down scenes were taken by C.B.A. helicopter.

Most of the streetlights were out. Those left intact cast monstrous shadows through the mall. Orange flames flickered in the windows of a furniture store. Diminutive figures, angered by spotlights in the helicopter, pointed and shouted silently into the camera viewpoint.

Digital transcription of the news anchor's words scrolled across the bottom of the screen: *We are getting no transmissions from inside the affected area. A dozen C.B.A. newsmen and an undisclosed number of police in the area have not been heard from.*

Many of the rioters are armed. A C.B.A. helicopter was shot down early today but was able to crash-land beyond the perimeter—footage showed a close-up image of a helicopter smashed against a brick wall and two men being carried out on stretchers, in obvious haste—*The source of weapons is not known. Police conjecture that they may have been looted from Kerr's Sport Shop, which has a branch in the mall.*

The square brown face looking out of the screen was known throughout the English-speaking world: Wash Evans.

When news was good, Wash would smile enormously.

He was not smiling now. His expression was more earnest—shaken.

Jerryberry Jansen looked back with no expression at all. He had thrown away his camera and seen it destroyed. He had dropped his coin purse and ear phone into a trash can. Not being a newstaper was a *good* idea during the mall riot.

Now, an hour after the police had let him through, he was still wandering aimlessly. He had no goal. Almost, he had thrown away his identity.

He stood in front of a pawn store window, watching through the cracked, wire-reinforced glass.

How did it all start? Wash asked.

Evans's face vanished, and Jerryberry watched scenes taken by his own camera: a milling crowd, mostly trying to get past a disturbance—a uniformed man, and a brawny woman with a heavy purse.

The officer was trying to arrest a suspected shoplifter, who has not been identified, when this man appeared on the scene.

Jerryberry saw an image of himself, camera held high, caught in the view of another, different C.B.A. camera.

Barry Jerome Jansen, a roving newstaper. It was he who reported the disturbance—

The woman swung her purse. The policeman went down, his arms half-raised as if to hide his head.

—and reported it as a riot, to this man—

Jerryberry's boss, at his desk in the C.B.A. building.

Jerryberry twitched. Sooner or later he would have to report to Bailey. And explain where his camera had gone.

He'd picked up some good footage, and it was being used. A string of bonuses waiting for him … unless he got docked for the cost of the camera.

George Bailey had sent in a whole crew to cover the disturbance. He had also put the report on cable and satellite—practically live, editing it as it came. At that point anyone with a television, anywhere in the United States, could see the violence being filmed by a dozen veteran C.B.A. newstapers.

The square dark face of Wash Evans returned.

—and then it all blew up. The population of the mall expanded catastrophically. To understand why, we have to consider who these people were.

Wash Evans had long, expressive fingers with pink nails. He began ticking off items on his fingers.

First, more police, to stop what was being reported as a riot. Second, more newstapers. Third, anyone who wanted publicity.

On the screen behind Wash Evans, signs shot out of a sea of moving heads. A girl's face swelled enormously, so close she seemed all mouth, and shrieked, "Legalize wireheading!"

Wash had it. Anyone with a cause. Anyone who wanted the ear of the public. There were newspeople! And cameras! And publicity!

Behind Evans the scene jumped. That was Angela Monk coming out of a displacement booth. Angela Monk—the popular porno movie actress with her own reality show, looking very beautiful in a dress of loose-mesh net made from white braided yarn. She seemed self-possessed for the split second it took her to figure out what she'd flicked into.

Then she tried to dodge back inside—to hell with the free coverage.

Male hands pulled the booth door open before she could dial again; other male hands pulled her out.

Jerryberry shuddered. How could this happen? This wasn't Syria or Egypt. It was California!

Wash kept speaking, his words printed on the screen in white letters.

Then there are people who have never seen a riot in person. A lot of them came. What they think about it now is … something else again.

Taken as a whole, these "disturbance tourists" might be a small percentage of the public—how many people are adventurous enough to come watch a riot? But that little percentage, they all came at once, from all over the United States—and some other places, too. And the more there were, the bigger the crowd got, the louder it got—and the better it looked to the looters.

Scenes shifted in Evans's background: store windows being smashed, a subdued wail of sirens, a C.B.A. helicopter thrashing about in midair, an ape of a man carrying stolen LCDs under one arm …

Evans looked soberly out at his audience.

So there you have it. An unidentified shoplifting suspect, a roving newsman who reported a minor disturbance as a riot—

"Good God!" Jerryberry Jansen exclaimed, suddenly coming completely awake. "They're blaming me!"

"They're blaming me, too," said George Bailey. He ran his hands through his glossy, shoulder-length, white hair that grew in a fringe around a dome of suntanned scalp. "You're second in the chain. I'm tired. If only they could find the woman who hit the cop!"

"They haven't?"

"Not a sign of her. Jansen, you look like hell."

"I should have changed suits. This one's been through a riot." Jerryberry's laugh sounded forced, and was. "I'm glad you waited. It must be way past your quitting time."

"Oh, no. We've been in conference all night. We only broke up about twenty minutes ago. Damn Wash Evans anyway! Have you heard—"

"I saw and read some of it."

"A couple of the directors want to fire him. Not unlike the ancient technique of using gasoline to put out a fire. There were some even wilder suggestions ... have you seen a doctor?"

"I'm not hurt. Just bruised ... and tired, and hungry, come to think of it. I lost my camera."

"You're lucky you got out alive."

"I know."

George Bailey seemed to brace himself. "I hate to be the one to tell you. We're going to have to let you go, Jansen."

"What? You mean fire me?" Jerryberry's stomach sank like a rock that's been dropped into the ocean. He'd worked too damned hard to get to where he was, and had too many plans to move up in the C.B.A. food chain. But what could he do? The politics of the situation were irrefutable.

"Yah," George said in a pained tone. "Public pressure. I won't make it pretty for you. Wash Evans's instant documentary has sort of torn things open. It seems you caused the mall riot. It would be nice if we could say we fired you for it."

"But—but I didn't!" Jerryberry exclaimed.

"Yes, you did. And so did I, in a way. I'm the guy who approved and fed your uncensored footage for livestreaming and live television. C.B.A. may have to fire me too."

"Now—" Jerryberry stopped and started over. "Now wait a minute. If you're saying what I think you're saying ... but what about freedom of the press?"

"We talked about that, too."

"I didn't exaggerate what was happening," Jerryberry said defensively. "I reported a—a disturbance. When it turned into a riot, I called it a riot. Did I lie about anything? Anything??"

"Oh, in a way," Bailey said in a tired voice. "You've got your choice about where to point that camera. You pointed it where there was fighting, didn't you? And I picked out the most exciting scenes. When we both finished, it looked like a small riot. Fighting everywhere! Then everyone who wanted to be in the middle of a small riot came flicking in, just like Evans said, and in thirty seconds we had a large riot.

"You know what somebody suggested? A time limit on news. A law against reporting anything until twenty-four hours after it happens. Can you imagine anything sillier? For ten thousand years the human race has been working to send news farther and faster, and now. ... Oh, hell, Jansen, I don't know about freedom of the press. But the riot's still going on, and everyone's blaming you. You're fired."

"Thanks," Jerryberry said, deadpan.

Angry as well as defeated, Jerryberry surged out of his chair on what felt like the last of his strength. Bailey moved just as fast, but by the time he got around the desk, Jerryberry was inside a booth, dialing.

Jerryberry stepped out into a warm black night. He felt sick and miserable and very tired. It was two in the morning. His suit was torn and crumpled and clammy.

George Bailey stepped out of the booth behind him.

"Thought so. Now, Jansen, let's talk sense."

"How did you know I'd be here?"

"I had to guess you'd come straight home. Jansen, you won't suffer for this. You may make money on it. C.B.A. wants an exclusive interview on the riot, your viewpoint. Thirty-five thousand bucks."

"Screw that."

"In addition, there's two weeks' severance pay and a stack of other bonuses. We used a lot of your footage. And when this blows over, I'm sure we'll want you back. On the hush-hush, of course."

"Blows over, huh?"

"Oh, it will. News gets stale awfully fast these days. I know, Jansen, why don't you want thirty-five thousand bucks?"

"You'd play me up as the man who started the mall riot. Make me more valuable ... wait a minute. Who have you got in mind for the interview?"

"Who else?"

"Wash Evans!"

"He's fair. You'd get your say. Let me know if you change your mind. You'd have a chance to defend yourself, and you'd get paid handsomely besides."

"No chance."

"All right."

Bailey went.

-3-

JERRYBERRY FUMED.

The words of his father came back to haunt him: *falling on your face can happen anytime, anywhere.*

For Eric Jansen and his family, displacement booths came as a disaster.

At first dad hadn't seen it that way. He was twenty-eight (and Barry Jerome Jansen was three) when JumpShift, Inc., demonstrated the augmented tunnel diode effect on a lead brick. Dad had watched the technological debut on television, and found the prospect exciting. Or so he'd often said.

But Eric Jansen had never worked for a salary. At that time, everything came through grandpa's estate. So dad wrote. Poetry and articles and a few short stories, highly polished, admired by a small circle of readers, sold at infrequent intervals to low-paying markets that dad regarded as prestigious. It hadn't mattered to dad if his work brought in large sums of cash. His money came from inherited stocks. If he had invested in JumpShift then ... but millions could tell that sad story.

Eric Jansen had considered it too much of a risk.

Dad was thirty-one when commercial displacement booths began to be sold for cargo transport. He was not caught napping. Many did not believe that the magic could work

45

until suddenly the phenomenon was changing their world. But Eric Jansen looked into the phenomenon very carefully.

He found that there was an inherent limitation on the augmented tunnel diode effect. Teleportation over a difference in altitude made for drastic temperature changes: a drop of seven degrees Fahrenheit for every mile upward, and vice versa, due to conservation of energy.

Conservation of momentum, plus the rotation of the Earth, put a distance limit on lateral travel. A passenger flicking east would find himself kicked upward by the difference between his velocity and the Earth's. Flicking west, he would be slapped down. North and south, he would be kicked sideways.

Cargo and passenger displacement booths were springing up in every city in America, but Eric Jansen knew that they would always be restricted to short distances. Even a ten-mile jump would be bumpy. A passenger flicking halfway around the equator would have to land running—at half a mile per second.

JumpShift stock was sky-high. Dad decided it must be overpriced.

He considered carefully, then made his move.

Eric Jansen sold all of his General Telephone stock. If anyone wanted to talk to someone, he would just go, wouldn't he? A displacement booth took no longer than a phone call.

He tried to sell his General Motors, wisely, but everyone else wisely made the same decision, and the price fell like a dead bird. At least he got something back on the stock he owned in motorcycle and motorscooter companies. Later he regretted that. It developed that people rode motorcycles and scooters for fun. Now, with the streets virtually empty, they were buying more than ever.

Still, Eric Jansen had fluid cash—and the opportunity to make a killing.

Airline stock had dropped with other forms of transportation. Before the general public could realize its mistake, dad invested every dime in airlines and aircraft companies. The first displacement booths in any city were links to the airport. That lousy half-hour drive from the center of town, the heavy taxi fare in, were gone forever. And the booths couldn't compete with the airlines themselves!

Of course you still had to check in early—and the planes took off only at specified times.

What it amounted to was that plane travel was made easier, but short-distance travel via displacement booth was infinitely easier (infinitely—try dividing any ten-minute drive by zero). And planes still crashed. DVDs and livestreaming had copped the entertainment market, so that television was mostly reality shows and news these days. You didn't have to go anywhere to find out what was happening. Just turn on the TV.

A plane flight wasn't worth the hassle.

As for the telephone stock, people still made long-distance calls. They tended to phone first before they went visiting. They would give out a phone-booth number, whereas they would not give out a displacement booth number.

The airlines survived, somehow, but they paid rock-bottom dividends.

Barry Jerome Jansen had therefore grown up poor in the midst of a boom economy. Dad hated the displacement booths but used them, because there was nothing else.

Jerryberry had grudgingly accepted dad's irrational hatred as part of his father's overall dour personality. But Jerryberry did not share it. He hardly noticed the displacement booths. They were part of the background of existence. Like wallpaper. The displacement booths were the most important part of a newstaper's life, and still Jerryberry hardly noticed their existence.

Until the day they turned on him.

-4-

In the morning there were messages stored in Jerryberry's cell phone voice mail. He heard them out over breakfast.

Half a dozen news services and profile programs wanted exclusives on the riot. One call was from Bailey at C.B.A. The price had gone up to forty thousand dollars. The others did not mention price, but one was from a politics blog—known for paying high, and liking unpopular causes.

Three people wanted to murder Jerryberry.

On two of them the picture was blanked. The third was a graying dowdy woman, all fat and hate and disappointed hopes, who showed him a kitchen knife and started to tell him what she wanted to do with it.

Jerryberry cut her off, shuddering. He wondered if any of them could possibly get hold of his displacement booth number.

There was an electronic deposit notice in e-mail: severance pay and bonuses from C.B.A., as Bailey had promised.

And so, that was that.

Jerryberry was setting the dishes in the dishwasher when the phone rang. He hesitated, then decided to answer.

It was Janice Wolfe—a pretty oval face, brown eyes, a crown of long, wavy, soft brown hair—and not an anonymous killer. She lost her smile as she saw him. "You look grim. Could you use some cheering up?"

"Yes!" Jerryberry said fervently. "Come on over. Apartment six, booth number—"

"I live here, remember?"

He laughed. He'd forgotten. You got used to people living anywhere and everywhere. George Bailey lived in Nevada; he commuted to work every morning in three flicks, using the long-distance displacement booths at Las Vegas and Los Angeles International Airports.

Those long-distance booths had saved the airlines—after his father had dribbled away most of his stocks to feed his family. They had been operating only two years. And come to think of it—

Doorbell.

Over coffee Jerryberry told Janice about the riot. She listened sympathetically, asking occasional questions to draw him out. At first he tried to talk entertainingly, until he realized, first, that she wasn't indulging in a spectator sport, and second, that she knew all about the riot already. She knew he'd been fired, too.

"That's why I called," she said. "They put it on the morning news."

"It figures."

"What are you going to do now?"

"Get drunk. Alone if I have to. Would you like to spend a lost weekend with me?"

She hesitated. "You'll be bitter."

"Yah, I probably will. Not fit to live with ... hey, Janice. Do you know anything about how the long-distance displacement booths work?"

"No. Should I?"

"The mall riot couldn't have happened without the long-distance booths. That damn Wash Evans might at least have mentioned the fact ... except that I only just thought of it myself. Funny. There hasn't ever been a riot that happened that quick."

"I'll come with you," Janice decided.

"What? Good."

"You don't start drinking this early in the morning, do you?"

"I guess not. Are you free today?"

"Every day, during summer. I teach school."

"Oh. So what'll we do? San Diego Zoo?" he suggested at random.

"Sounds like fun."

They made no move to get up. It felt peaceful in Jerryberry's tiny kitchen nook. There was still coffee.

"You could get a bad opinion of me this way. I feel like tearing things up."

"Go ahead."

"Mean it?"

"Me, too," she said serenely. "You need to tear things up. Fine, go ahead. After that you can try to put your life back together."

"Just what kind of school do you teach?"

Janice laughed. "Fifth grade."

There was quiet.

"You know what the punch line is? Wash Evans wants to *interview* me. After that speech he made!"

"That sounds like a good idea," she said surprisingly. "Gives you a chance to give your side of the story. You didn't really cause the mall riot, did you?"

"No! ... no. Janice, he's just too damn good. He'd make mincemeat of me. By the time he got through I'd be The Man Who Caused the Mall Riot in every English-speaking country in the world, and some others, too, because he gets translations—"

"He's just a pundit."

Jerryberry started to laugh.

"He makes it look so easy," Jerryberry said. "A hundred million eyes out there, watching Wash, and he knows it. Have you ever seen him self-conscious? Have you ever heard him at a loss for words? My dad used to say it about writing, but it's true for Wash Evans. The hardest trick in the world is to make it look easy, so easy that any clod thinks he can do it just as well.

"Hell, I know what caused the mall riot. The news program, yes. He's right, there. But the long-distance displacement booth did it, too. Control those, and we could stop that kind of riot from ever happening again. But what could I tell Wash Evans about it? What do I know about displacement booths?"

"Well, what do you know?"

Jerryberry Jansen looked into his coffee cup for a long time. Presently he said, "I know how to find out things. I know how to find out who knows most about what and then go ask. Legwork. I *know* legwork."

He looked up and met her eyes. Then he lunged across the table to reach for his cell phone.

"Hello? Oh, hi, Jansen. Changed your mind?" said George Bailey's voice.

"Yes, but—" Jerryberry began.

"Good, good! I'll put you through to—"

"Yes, but—!" Jerryberry almost yelled.

"Oh. Okay, go ahead."

"I want some time to do some research."

"Now, damn it, Jensen, you know that time is just what we don't have. Old news is *no* news. What kind of research?"

"Displacement booths."

"Why that? Never mind—it's your business. How much time?"

"How much can you afford?"

"Damn little."

"Bailey, C.B.A. upped my price to forty thousand this morning. How come?"

"You didn't see it? It's on every screen in the country. The rioters broke through the police line. They've got a good section of Venice now, and there are about twice as many of them, because the police didn't shut down the displacement booths in the area until about twenty minutes too late.

Twenty minutes!" Bailey seemed actually to be grinding his teeth. "We held off reporting the breakthrough until they could do it. We did. A.B.S. reported it live on all their stations. That's where all the new rioters came from."

"Then … it looks like the mall riot is going to last a little longer."

"That it does. And you want more time. Things are working out, aren't they?" Then, "Sorry. Those A.B.S. bastards. How much time do you want?"

"As much as I can get. A week."

"You've got to be kidding. You maybe can get twenty-four hours, only I can't make the decision. Why don't you talk to Evans himself?"

"Fine. Put him on."

The phone went on hold. Pale-blue flow patterns floated upward in what had become a tiny kaleidoscope on Jerryberry's phone screen.

Waiting, Jerryberry said, "If this riot gets any bigger, I could be more famous than Hitler."

Janice set his coffee beside him. She said, "… or Mrs. O'Leary's cow."

"Who?"

Janice rolled her eyes at him.

The screen came back on. "Jansen, can you get over here right now? Wash Evans wants to talk to you in person."

"Okay." Jerryberry clicked off. He felt a thrumming inside him … as if he felt the motion of the world, and the world were spinning faster and faster. Surely things were happening *too* fast. But he had to take action, or risk losing everything he'd worked for in his life.

Janice said, "No lost weekend?"

"Not yet, love. Have you any idea what you've let me in for? I may not sleep for days. I'll have to find out what teleportation is, what it does. Where do I start?"

"Wash Evans. You'd better get moving."

"Right." Jerryberry gulped his coffee in three swift swallows. "Thanks. Thanks for coming over, thanks for jarring me off the dime. We'll see how it works out." He went to Janice and gave her a quick hug, which she returned with a startled laugh. Then he was out the door, pulling on a coat.

Wash Evans was five feet four inches tall. People sometimes forgot that size was invisible before the camera eye. In the middle of a televised interview, when the picture was flashing back and forth between two angry faces, then the deep, sure voice and the dark, mobile, expressive face of Wash Evans could be devastatingly convincing.

Wash Evans looked up at Jerryberry Jansen and said, "I've been wondering if I owe you an apology."

"Take your time," said Jerryberry. He finished buttoning his coat.

"I don't. Fact is, I psyched out the mall riot as best I knew how, and I think I did it right. I didn't tell the great unwashed public you caused it all. I just told it like it happened."

"You left some things out."

"All right, now we've got something to talk about. Sit down." They sat. Their faces were level now. Jerryberry said, "This present conversation is not for publication and is not to be considered an interview. I have an interview to sell. I don't want to undercut myself."

"I accept your terms on behalf of the network. We'll give you a digital copy of this conversation."

"I'm making my own." Jerryberry tapped his inside pocket, which clicked.

Wash Evans grinned. "Of course you are, my child. Now, what did I miss?"

"Displacement booths."

"Well, sure. If the booths had been cut off earlier—"

"If the booths didn't exist."

"You're kidding ... no, you're *not*. Jansen, that's a wishing horse. Displacement booths are here to stay."

"I know. But think about this. Newstapers have been around longer than displacement booths. Roving newstapers, like me—we've been using the booths since they were invented."

"So?"

"Why didn't the mall riot happen earlier?"

"I see what you mean. Hmm. The airport booths. Jansen, are you actually going to face the great unwashed public and tell them to give up long-distance displacement booths?"

"No. I … don't know just what I have in mind. That's why I want some time. I want to know more."

"Uh-huh," said Evans, and waited.

Jerryberry said, "Turn it around. Are you going to try to talk the public into giving up news programs?"

"No. Maybe to put some restrictions on newstaping practices. We're too fast these days. A machine won't work without friction. Neither does a civilization … but we'd ruin the networks, wouldn't we?"

"You'd cut your own throat."

"Oh, I'd probably be out." Evans said, smiling sardonically. "Take away the news broadcasts, and they wouldn't have anything left to sell but reality shows, with commercials for toys and breakfast cereals."

Evans's expression grew more grim. "Look, Jansen, I don't *know*."

"Good," said Jerryberry.

Evans sat up a little straighter. "You question my dispassionate judgment? I'm on both sides. Suppose we do an interview live, at ten tonight. That'll give you twelve hours—"

"Twelve hours!" Jerryberry said loudly.

"That's enough, isn't it? You want to research teleportation. I want to get this in while people are still interested in the riot. Not just for the ratings, but because we both have something to say."

Jerryberry tried to interrupt, but Evans overrode him.

"We'll advance you five thousand now, and five more if we do the interview *tonight*. Guaranteed. You get nothing if we don't. That'll get you back on time, if nothing else will."

Jerryberry wanted to tell Wash Evans to go to hell. But he accepted the terms.

"One thing," Jerryberry said. "Can you make Bailey forget to cancel my C.B.A. card for a while? I may have to do a lot of traveling."

"I'll tell him. I don't know if he'll do it. But I'll tell him."

-5-

JERRYBERRY FLICKED IN at Los Angeles International, off-center in a long curved row of displacement booths: upright glass cylinders with rounded tops, no different from the booths on any street corner. On the opposite wall, a good distance away, large letters said DELTA.

Jerryberry stood a moment, thinking. Then he dialed again.

He was home, at the Shady Rest. He dialed again.

He was near the end of the row—a different row, with no curve to it. And the opposite wall bore the emblem of AMERICAN.

The terminal was empty except for one man in a blue uniform who was waxing the floor.

Jerryberry stepped out. For upwards of a minute he watched the line of booths. People flicked in at random. Generally they did not even look up. They would dial a long string of digits—sometimes making a mistake, snarling something, and starting over—and be gone. There were so many that the booths themselves seemed to be flickering.

He took several seconds of it on his personal Minox digital camera.

Beneath the American Airlines emblem was a long, long row of empty counters with scales between them, for luggage.

56

The terminal was spotless—and empty, unused. Haunted by a constant flow of ghosts.

A voice behind him said, "You want something?"

"Is there a manager's office?" Jerryberry asked.

The uniformed man pointed down an enormous length of corridor. "The maintenance section's down that way, where the boarding area used to be. I'll call ahead, let them know you're coming."

The corridor was long, unnecessarily long, and it echoed. The walk was eating up valuable time … and then an open cart came from the other end and silently pulled up alongside him. A straight-backed old man in a one-button business lounger said, "Hello. Want a ride?"

"Thanks." Jerryberry climbed aboard. He handed over his C.B.A. credit card. "I'm doing some research for a—a documentary of sorts. What can you tell me about the long-distance booths?"

"Anything you like. I'm Nils Kjerulf. I helped install these booths, and I've been working on them ever since."

"How do they work?"

"Where do I start? Do you know how a normal booth works?"

"Sure. The load isn't supposed to exist at all between the two endpoints. Like the electron in a tunnel diode." An answer right out of Popular Mechanics. Beyond that … Jerryberry could fake it.

Nils Kjerulf was lean and ancient, with deep smile wrinkles around his eyes and mouth. His hair was thick and white. He said, "They had to give up that theory. When you're sending a load to Mars, say, you have to assume that something exists in the ten minutes or so it takes the load to make the trip. Conservation of energy."

"All right. What is it?"

"For ten minutes it's a kind of superneutrino. That's what they tell me. I'm not a physicist. I was in business administration in college. A few years ago they gave me a year of retraining so I could handle long-distance displacement machinery. If you're really interested in theory, you ought to ask someone at Cape Canaveral. Here we are."

Two escalators, one going up, one motionless. They rode up. Jerryberry asked, "Why didn't they build closer? Think of all the walking we'd save."

"You never heard an A380 taking off?"

"No."

"Sound is only part of it. If a plane ever crashed here, no-body would want it hitting all the main buildings at once."

The escalator led to two semicircular chambers. One was empty but for a maze of chairs and couches and low partitions, all done in old chrome and fading orange. In the other the couches had been ripped out and replaced with instrument consoles. Jerryberry counted half a dozen men supervising the displays.

A dim snoring sound began somewhere, like an electric razor going in the next-door apartment. Jerryberry turned his head, seeking. It was outside. Outside, behind a wall of windows, a tiny single-engine plane taxied down a runway.

"Yes, we still function as an airport," said Nils Kjerulf. "Skydiving, sport flying, gliding. I fly some myself. The jumbo-jet pilots used to hate us; we use up just as much landing time as a 777. Now we've got the runways to ourselves."

"I gather you were a manager somewhere."

"Right here. I ran this terminal before anyone had heard of teleportation. I watched it ruin us. Thirty years, Mr. Jansen."

"With no offense intended," Jerryberry said, "why did they train a professional administrator in quantum displacement physics? Why not the other way around?"

"There weren't any experts where the long-distance booths were concerned, Mr. Jansen. They're new."

"What have you learned in two years? Do you still get many breakdowns?"

"We still do. Every two weeks or so, something goes out of synch. Then we go out of service for however long it takes to find it and fix it—usually about an hour."

"And what happens to the passenger?"

Kjerulf looked surprised. "Nothing. He stays where he started—or rather, that giant neutrino we were talking about is reflected back to the transmitter if the receiver can't pick it up. The worst thing that can happen is that the link to the velocity damper could be lost, in which case—but we've developed safeguards against that.

"No, the passengers just stop coming in, and we go out of service, and the other companies take the overflow. There isn't any real competition between the companies anymore. What's the point? Delta and United and American and all the rest used to advertise that they had more comfortable seats, better leg room, in-flight wifi … stuff like that. How long do you spend in a displacement booth? So when we converted over, we set the dialing system up so you just dial Los Angeles International or whatever, and the companies get customers at random. Everyone saves a fortune in advertising."

"An antitrust suit—"

"Would have us dead to rights. Nobody's done it, because there's no point. It works, the way we run it. Each company has its own velocity shift damper. We couldn't all get knocked out at once. In an emergency I think any of the companies could handle all of the long-distance traffic."

"Mr. Kjerulf, what is a velocity shift damper?"

Kjerulf looked startled.

Jerryberry said, "I'm a newstaper, not an engineer."

"Ah," Kjerulf said.

"It's not just curiosity. My dad lost a fortune on airline stock—"

"So did I," said Kjerulf, half-smiling with old pain.

"Oh?"

"Sometimes I feel I've sold out. The booths couldn't possibly compete with the airlines, could they? They wouldn't send far enough. Yet they ruined us."

"My dad figured the same way."

"And now the booths do send that far, and I'm working for them, or they're working for me. There wasn't all that much reason to build the long-distance systems at airports. Lots of

59

room here, of course, and an organization already set up ... but they really did it to save the airline companies."

"A little late."

"Perhaps. Some day they'll turn us into a public utility." Kjerulf looked about the room, then called to a man seated near the flat wall of the semicircle. "Dan!"

"Yo!" the man boomed without looking up.

"Can you spare me twenty minutes for a public-relations job?"

Dan stood up, then climbed up on his chair. He looked slowly about the room—Jerryberry guessed Dan could see every instrument board from where he was standing.

Dan called, "Sure. No sweat."

They took the cart back to the terminal. They entered a booth. Jerryberry inserted his C.B.A. credit card, then waited while Kjerulf dialed.

They were in a concrete building. Beyond large square windows a sunlit sea of blue water heaved and splashed, almost at floor level. Men looked around curiously, recognized Nils Kjerulf, and turned back to their work.

"Lake Michigan. And out there"—Kjerulf pointed; Jerryberry saw a tremendous white mass, like a flattened dome, very regular, forming a softly rounded island—"is the United Air Lines velocity damper. All of the dampers look about like that, but they float in different lakes or oceans. Aeroflot uses the Caspian Sea. The Delta damper is in the Gulf of Mexico."

"Just what is it?"

"Essentially it's a hell of a lot of soft iron surrounded by a hell of a lot more foam plastic, enough to float it, plus a displacement-booth receiver feeding into the iron. Look, see it surge?"

The island rose several feet, slowly, then fell back as slowly. Ripples moved outward and became waves as they reached the station.

"That must have been a big load," Kjerulf said. "Now, here's how it works. You know that the rotation of the Earth puts a limit on how far you can send a load. If you were to shift from here to Rio de Janeiro, say, you'd flick in moving up and sideways—mainly up, because Rio and L.A. are almost the same distance from the equator.

"But with the long-distance booths, the receiver picks up the kinetic energy and shunts it to the United Air Lines velocity damper. That big mass of iron surges up or down or sideways until the water stops it—or someone flicks in from Rio and the damping body stops cold."

Jerryberry thought about it. "What about conservation of rotation? It sounds like you're slowing down the Earth."

"We are. There's nothing sacred about conservation of rotation, except that the energy has to go somewhere. There are pumps to send water through the damper bodies if they get too hot."

Jerryberry pulled out the digital Minox. "Mind if I take some pictures?"

"No, go ahead."

Jerryberry took shots of the men at work in the station, of Nils Kjerulf with his back to the windows. He shot almost a minute of hi-res featuring the great white island itself. He was hoping it would surge; and presently it did, sinking sideways, surging up again. Waves beat at the station. A jet of white steam sprayed from the top of the great white mass.

"Good," Jerryberry said briskly to himself. He folded the spidery tripod legs and dropped the camera in his pocket. He turned to Kjerulf, who had been watching the proceedings with some amusement. "Mr. Kjerulf, can you tell me anything about traffic control? Is there any?"

"How do you mean? Customs?"

"Not exactly ... but tell me about customs."

"The customs terminal in Los Angeles is at Delta. You haven't been out of the country recently? No? Well, any big-city airport has a customs terminal. In a small country there's likely to be just one. If you dial a number outside the country, any country, you wind up in somebody's customs terminal.

The booths there don't have dials, you see. You have to cross the customs line to dial out."

"Clever. Are there any restrictions on traffic within the United States?"

"No, you just swipe your card, or drop your dollars in, and dial. Unless it's a police matter. If the police know that someone's trying to leave the city they may set up a watch in the terminals. We can put a delay on the terminals to give a detective time to look at a passenger's face and see if he's who they want."

"But nothing to stop passengers from coming in."

"No, except that it's possible to …" Kjerulf trailed off oddly, then finished, "… turn *off* any booth by remote control, from the nearest JumpShift maintenance system. What are you thinking of, the mall riot?"

There was no more to say. Jerryberry left Nils Kjerulf in the United terminal in Los Angeles. He dialed for customs.

For several minutes Jerryberry watched them flicking in. There were two types:

The tourists came in couples, sometimes with a child or two. They flicked in looking interested and harried and a little frightened. Their clothing was outlandish and extraordinary. Before they left the booths, they would look about them mistrustfully. Sometimes they formed larger groups.

The businessmen traveled alone. They wore conservative or old-fashioned clothing and carried one suitcase: large or small, but one. They were older than the tourists. They moved with authority, walking straight out of the booths the moment they appeared.

At the barrier: four men in identical dark suits with shield-shaped shoulder patches.

Jerryberry was on the wrong side of the barrier to command their attention. He was thinking of dialing himself to Mexico and back when one of them noticed him and pegged him as a newstaper.

His name was Gregory Scheffer. Small and round and middle-aged, he perched on the steel barrier and clasped one knee in both hands. "Sure, I can talk a while. This isn't one of the busy days. The only time these booths really get a work-out is Christmas and New Year's and Bastille Day and stuff like that. Look around you," he said, waving a pudgy hand expansively.

"About four times as many incoming as there was six months ago. I used to want to search every bag that came through, just to be doing something. If we keep getting more and more of them this way, we'll need twice as many customs people next year."

"Why do you suppose—"

"Did you know that the long-distance booths have been operating for two solid years? It's only in the last six months or so that we've started to get so many passengers. They had to get used to traveling again. Look around you; look at all this space. It used to be full before JumpShift came along. People have got out of the habit of traveling, that's all there is to it. For twenty solid years. They have to get back into it."

"Guess so." Jerryberry tried to remember why he was here. "Mr. Scheffer—"

"Greg."

"Jerryberry. Customs' main job is to stop smuggling, isn't it?"

"Well ... it used to be. Now we only slow it down, and not very damn much. Nobody in his right mind would smuggle anything through customs. There are safer ways."

"Oh?"

"Diamonds, for instance. Diamonds are practically inde-structible. You could rig a cargo booth in Kansas to receive from ... oh, there's a point in the South Pacific to match any-place in the United States: same longitude, opposite latitude. You don't need a velocity damper if you put the boat in the right place. Diamonds? You could ship in Swiss watches that way. Though that's pretty finicky. You'd want to pad them."

"Good grief. You could smuggle anything you pleased, anywhere."

"Just about. You don't need the ocean trick. Say you rig a booth a mile south of the Canadian border, and another booth a mile north. That's not much of a jump. You can flick further than that just in L.A. I think we're obsolete," said Scheffer. "I think smuggling laws are obsolete. You won't publish this?"

"I won't use your name."

"I guess that's okay."

"Can you get me over to the incoming booths? I want to take some pictures."

"What for?"

"I'm not sure yet."

"Let's see some ID." Gregory Scheffer didn't trust evasive answers. The incoming booths were in his jurisdiction. He studied the C.B.A. card for a few seconds and suddenly said, "Jansen! Mall riot!"

"Right," Jerryberry said reluctantly.

"What was it like?"

Jerryberry invested half a minute telling him. "So now I'm trying to find out how it got started. If there were some way to stop all of those people from pouring in like that—"

"You won't find it here. Look, a dozen passengers and we're almost busy. A thousand people suddenly pour through those booths, and what would we do? Hide under something, that's what we'd do."

"I still want to see the incoming booths."

Scheffer thought it over, shrugged, and let him through. He stood at Jerryberry's shoulder while Jerryberry used his eye and his camera.

The booth was just like a street-corner booth, except for the blank metal face where a dial would be. "I don't know what's underneath," Scheffer told him. "For all of me, it's just like any other booth. How much work would it be to leave off the dial?"

Which made sense. But it was no help at all.

-6-

THEY TAPED *The Tonight Show* at two in the afternoon.

Twenty minutes into it, the host was lolling at his ease, just rapping, talking off the top of his head, ignoring the probable millions of eyes that might be watching, either on cable, satellite, or the internet. The first guest played a popular series hero in one of the big comic book franchise films.

Striking face. Magnetic personality. A natural for the big screen.

He was saying, "Have you ever seen a red tide? It's thick down at Hermosa Beach. I was there this weekend. In the daytime it's just dirty water, muddy-looking, and it smells. But at night ..."

The guest's enthusiasm was infectious. The kind of telegenic personal electricity that could reach through a screen to touch countless minds.

He leaned forward in his chair, eyes blazing.

"The breakers glow like churning blue fire! Those plankton are fluorescent. And they're all through the wet sand. Walk across it, it flashes blue light under your feet! Kick it, scuff your feet through it, it lights up. Throw a handful of sand, it flashes where it hits! This light isn't just on the surface. Stamp your foot, you can see the structure of the sand by the way it flares. You've got to see it to believe it."

The tape wouldn't run until eight thirty.

-7-

JERRYBERRY TAPPED NOTES onto his digital pad.

Standard booths: how standardized?

Who makes them besides JumpShift? Monopoly? How extensive? Skip spaceflight?

Space exploration depended utterly on teleportation. But the subject was likely to be very technical and not very useful. He could gain time by skipping it entirely.

Jerryberry considered, then turned the question mark into an exclamation point.

His twelve hours had become nine.

Of the half-dozen key clubs to which Jerryberry belonged, the Cave des Roys was the quietest. A place of stone and wood, a good place to sit and think. The wall behind the bar was several hundred wine bottles in a cement matrix. Jerryberry looked into the strange lights in the glass, sipped occasionally at a silver fizz, and jotted down whatever occurred to him.

Sociology. What has teleportation done to society?

Cars.

Oil companies. Oil stocks. See back issues: Wall Street Journal.

Watts riot? Chicago riot? L.A. riot? New Orleans?

He crossed that last one out. It had been a natural disaster, more than a riot.

Then Jerryberry couldn't remember any other riots. They were too far in the past. He wrote:

Riot control. Police procedure.

Crime? The crime rate should have soared after displacement booths provided the instant getaway. But *had* it?

Sooner or later Jerryberry was going to have to drop in at police headquarters. He'd hate that, but he might learn something. Likewise the library, for several hours of dull research. Then?

He certainly wasn't going to persuade everybody to give up displacement booths.

Jerryberry wrote: *OBJECTIVE—demonstrate that displacement booths imply instant riot. It's a social problem. Solve it on that basis.*

For the sake of honesty he added, *Get 'em off my back.*

Next: *CROWDS—in minutes the mall had become a milling mass of men.*

But he'd seen crowds form almost as fast. It might happen regularly in certain places. After a moment's thought he wrote: *Tahiti. Jerusalem. Mecca. Easter Island. Stonehenge. Olduvai Gorge.*

Jerryberry stood up. Start with the phone calls.

"Doctor Robin Whyte," Jerryberry said to the phone's screen. "Please."

The receptionist at Seven Sixes was no sex symbol. She was old enough to be Jerryberry's aunt, and handsome rather than beautiful. She heard him out with a noncommittal dignity that, he sensed, could turn glacial in an instant.

"Barry Jerome Jansen," he said carefully.

He waited on hold, watching dark-red patterns flow upward in the phone screen.

Key clubs were neither new nor rare. Some were small and local; others were chains, existing in a dozen or a hundred locations. Everyone belonged to a club; most people belonged to several.

68

But Seven Sixes was something else. Its telephone number was known universally. Its membership, large in absolute terms, was small for an organization so worldwide. It included presidents, kings, winners of various brands of Nobel prize. Its location was—unknown. Somewhere in Earth's temperate zones. Jerryberry had never heard of its displacement booth number being leaked to anyone.

It took a special kind of gall for one of Jerryberry's social standing to dial 666-6666. He had learned that gall as a newstaper. Go to the source—no matter how highly placed. Be polite, be prepared to wait, but keep trying, and never, never worry about wasting the Great Man's time.

Funny. They still called newstaping *journalism*, though the major papers had died out. To be replaced by web media. And the Constitution that had protected papers still protected "the press," though nothing was physically pressed anymore. How long would that protection last? Laws could change. They had in the past. In response to technological innovation.

The screen cleared.

Robin Whyte the physicist had been a mature man of formidable reputation back when JumpShift first demonstrated teleportation. Today, twenty-five years later, he was the last living member of the team that had formed JumpShift. His scalp was pink and bare. His face was round and soft, almost without wrinkles, but slack, as if the muscles were tired. He looked like somebody's favorite grandfather.

He looked Jerryberry Jansen up and down very thoroughly. He said, "I wanted to see what you looked like. Hard to believe *you* are the man who caused the riot." Whyte reached for the cutoff button.

"I didn't do it," Jerryberry said quickly.

Whyte stopped with his finger on the cutoff. "No?"

"I am *not* responsible for what happened. I hope to prove it."

The old man thought it over. "And you propose to involve me? How?"

69

Jerryberry took a chance. "I think I can demonstrate that displacement booths and the mall riot are intimately connected. My problem is that I don't know enough about displacement booth technology."

"And you want my help?"

"You invented the displacement booths practically single-handed," Jerryberry said straight-faced. "Instant riots, instant getaways, instant smuggling. Are you going to just walk away from the problem?"

Robin Whyte laughed in a high-pitched voice, his head thrown way back, his teeth white and perfect and clearly false. Jerryberry waited, wondering if it would work.

"All right," Whyte said. "Come on over. Wait a minute, what am I thinking? You can't come to Seven Sixes. I'll meet you somewhere. L'Orangerie, New York City. At the bar."

The screen cleared before Jerryberry could answer. That was quick, he thought. And ... *move, idiot.* Get there before Whyte changes his mind!

In New York it was just approaching cocktail hour. L'Orangerie was polished wood and dim lighting and chafing dishes of Swedish meatballs on toothpicks. Jerryberry captured a few to go with his drink. He had not had lunch yet.

Dr. Whyte wore a long-sleeved gray one-piece with a collar that draped into a short cape, and the cape was all the shifting rainbow colors of an oil film—the height of haute, except that it should have been skin-tight. On Whyte it was loose all over, bagging where Whyte bagged, and it looked very comfortable. Whyte sipped at a glass of milk.

"One by one I give up my sins," he said. "Drinking was the last, and I haven't really turned loose of it yet. But almost. That's why your reverse salesmanship hooked me in. I'll talk to anyone. What do I call you?"

"Jerryberry."

Whyte laughed. "I can't call *anyone* Jerryberry."

"Barry Jerome Jansen."

"Make it just, 'Barry'?"

70

"God bless you, sir."

Whyte chuckled, and took another sip of milk.

"What do you want to know?"

"How big is JumpShift?"

"Ooohhh, pretty big. What's your standard of measurement?"

Jerryberry, who had wondered if he was being laughed at, stopped wondering. "How many kinds of booth do you make?"

"Hard to say. Three, for general use. Maybe a dozen more for the space industry. Those are still experimental. We lose money on the space industry. We'd make it back if we could start producing drop-ships in quantity. We've got a ship on the drawing boards that would transmit itself to any drop-ship receiver."

Jerryberry prompted him. "And three for general use, you said."

"Yes. We've made over three hundred million passenger booths in the past twenty years. Then there's a general-use cargo booth. The third model is a tremendous portable booth for shipping really big, fragile cargoes. Like a prefab house or a rocket booster or a live sperm whale. You can set the thing in place almost anywhere, using three strap-on helicopter setups. I didn't believe it when I saw it." Whyte sipped at his milk. "You've got to remember that I'm not in the business anymore. I'm still chairman of the board, but a bunch of younger people give most of the orders, and I hardly ever get into the factories."

"Does JumpShift have a monopoly on displacement booths?"

Jerryberry saw the *Newstaper*—*!* Reaction on Whyte's face: a tightening at the eyes and lips.

"Wrong word," Jerryberry said quickly. "Sorry. What I meant was, who *makes* displacement booths? I'm sure you make most of the passenger booths in the United States."

"All of them. It's not a question of monopoly. Anyone could make his own booths. Any community could. But it would be hideously expensive. The cost doesn't drop until you're making millions of them. So suppose … Chile, for instance. Chile has less than a million passenger booths, all JumpShift model. Suppose they had gone ahead and made their own. They'd have only their own network, unless they built a direct copy of some other model. All the booths in a network have to have the same volume."

"Naturally."

"In practice there are about ten networks worldwide. The European Union network is the biggest by far. I think the smallest is Brazil—"

"What happens to the air in a receiver?"

Whyte burst out laughing. "I knew that was coming! It never fails." He sobered. "We tried a lot of things. It turns out the only practical solution is to send the air in the receiver back to the transmitter, which means that every transmitter has to be a receiver, too."

"Then you could get a free ride if you knew who was about to flick in from where, when."

"Of course you could, but would you want to bet on it?"

"I might, if I had something to smuggle past customs."

"How do you mean?"

"I'm just playing with ideas. The incoming booths at customs are incoming because there's no way to dial out—"

"I remember now. Booth Type One, with the dial removed."

"Okay. Say you wanted to smuggle something into the country. You flick to customs in Argentina. Then a friend flicks from California to Argentina, into your booth. You wind up in his booth, in California, and not behind the customs barrier."

"Brilliant," said Whyte. "Unfortunately there's a fail-safe to stop anyone from flicking into an occupied booth."

"Ah."

"Sorry," Whyte said, grinning. "What do you care? There are easier ways to smuggle. Too many. I'm not really sorry. I'm a laissez-faire man myself."

"I wondered if you could do something with dials to stop another mall riot."

Whyte thought about it. "Not by taking the dials off. If you wanted to stop a riot, you'd have to stop people from coming in. Counters on the booths, maybe … uhh, Barry, honestly, what was it *like*?"

"Crowded," Jerryberry said, his gaze unfocused. "Like a dam broke. The law did shut the booths down from outside, but not fast enough. Maybe that's the answer. Cut out the booths at the first sign of trouble."

"We'd get a lot of people mad at us."

"You would, wouldn't you?"

"Like junk mail. Spammers. Are you old enough to remember that? For awhile you couldn't do anything about it, except get more and more uptight. More ready to smash things. I think that's why riots happen, Barry. Lots of people who are a little bit angry at the world all the time. Someone or something just has to light the fuse, and *boom*."

"Oh?"

"All the riots I remember," Whyte smiled. "There haven't been any for a long time. Give JumpShift some credit for that. We stopped some of the things that kept everyone a little bit angry all the time. Smog. Traffic jams. Slow deliveries. Slum landlords—you don't have to live near your job or your welfare office or whatever. Job hunting. Crowding. Have you ever been in a traffic jam?"

"Maybe when I was a little boy."

"Friend of mine was a college professor for a while. Seattle area. His problem was he lived in the wrong place. Five days a week he would spend two hours driving to work—you don't believe me?—and two hours and a quarter driving home; because traffic on Interstate 5 was heavier then. Eventually my friend gave it up to be a writer."

"God, I should hope so!"

"It wasn't even that rare," Whyte said seriously. "The whole west coast was like that. It was rough if you owned a

73

car, and rougher if you didn't. JumpShift didn't cause riots; we *cured* them."

And he seemed to wait for Jerryberry's agreement.

Silence stretched long enough to become embarrassing … yet the only thing Jerryberry might have said to break it was, *but what about the mall riot??*

Jerryberry held his peace. Whyte's mind appeared to be chewing on something.

"Drain that thing," Whyte then said abruptly. "I'll show you."

"Show me?"

"Finish that drink. We're going places." Whyte drank half a glass of milk in three gulps, his Adam's apple bobbing. He lowered the glass. "Well?"

"Ready."

On Madison Avenue the sunset shadows ran almost horizontally along the glass faces of buildings. Robin Whyte stepped out of L'Orangerie and turned right.

Four feet away, a displacement booth.

In the booth Whyte blocked the hand Jerryberry would have used to insert his C.B.A. card.

"My treat. This was my idea … anyway, some of these numbers are secret."

Whyte inserted his own card and dialed three numbers.

Twice they saw rows of long-distance booths. Then it was bright sunlight and sea breeze. Far out beyond a sandy beach and white waves, a great cylinder with a rounded top rose high out of the water. Orange letters on the curved metal flank read: JUMPSHIFT FRESHWATER TRANSPORT.

"I could take you out in a boat," said Whyte. "But it would be a waste of time. You wouldn't see much. Nothing but vacuum inside. You know how it works?"

"Sure."

"Teleportation was like laser technology. One big breakthrough and then a thousand ways to follow up on it. We spent twelve solid years building continuous teleport pumps for various municipalities to ship fresh water in various directions. When all the time the real problem was getting the fresh water, not moving it.

"Do you know how we developed this gimmick? My secretary dreamed it up one night at an office party. She was about half smashed, but she wrote it down, and the next morning we all took turns trying to read her handwriting. It's a simple idea. You build a tank, then put the teleport pump in the top. You teleport the air out. When the air goes, the seawater boils. From then on you're teleporting cold water vapor. It condenses wherever you ship it, and you get fresh water. Want to take pictures?"

"I do."

"Then let's look at the results," Whyte said, and dialed.

Now it was even brighter. The booth was backed up against a long wooden building. Far away was a white glare of salt flats, backed by blue ghosts of mountains. Jerryberry blinked and squinted. Whyte opened the door.

It hit them like a blast furnace.

Jerryberry said, "Whoooff!"

"Death Valley. Hot, isn't it?"

Jerryberry felt perspiration start as a rippling itch all over him. "I'm going to pretend I'm in a sauna. Speaking of which, why doesn't anyone ever put displacement booths inside their homes?"

"They did for a while. There were too many burglaries. Let's go around back."

They walked around the dry wooden building … and into an oasis. Jerryberry was jarred. On one side of the building, the austere beauty of a barren desert. On the other was a manicured forest: rows and rows of trees.

"We can grow damn near anything out here. We started with date palms, went to orange and grapefruit trees, pineapples, a lot of rice paddies, mangoes—anything that grows in tropical climates will grow here, as long as you give it enough water."

Jerryberry had already noticed the water tower. It looked just like the transmitter. He said, "And the right soil."

"Well, yes. Soil isn't that good in Death Valley. We have to haul in too much fertilizer." Rivulets of perspiration ran down Whyte's cheeks. His soft face looked almost stern. "But the principle holds. With teleportation, men can live practically anywhere. We gave people room. A man can work in Manhattan or Central Los Angeles or Central Anywhere and live in—in—"

"Nevada," Jerryberry finished for him.

"Or Hawaii!" Whyte exclaimed. "Or the Grand Canyon! Crowding caused riots. We've eliminated crowding."

Jerryberry considered keeping his mouth shut but decided he didn't have the willpower. "What about pollution?"

"What?"

"Death Valley used to have an ecology as unique as its climate. What's your unlimited water doing to that?"

"Ruining it, I guess."

"Hawaii, you said. Grand Canyon. There are laws against putting up apartment buildings in national monuments, thank God. Hawaii probably has the population density of New York by now. Your displacement booths can put men anywhere, right? Even places they don't belong."

"Well, maybe they can," Whyte said slowly. "Pollution. Hmm ... What do you know about Death Valley?"

"It's hot."

Jerryberry was wet through.

"Death Valley used to be an inland sea. A salt sea. Then the climate changed, and all the water went away. What did that do to the ecology?"

Jerryberry scratched his head. "A sea?"

"Yes, a sea! And drying it up ruined one ecology and started another, just like we're doing. But never mind that. I want to show you some things. Pollution, huh?" Whyte's grip on Jerryberry's arm was stronger than it had any right to be.

Whyte was angry. In the booth he froze, with his brow furrowed and his forefinger extended. Trying to remember a number. Then he dialed in trembling haste.

He dialed two sequences. Jerryberry saw the interior of an airline terminal, then—dark.

"Oh, damn. I forgot it would be night here."

"Where are we?"

"Sahara Desert. Rudolph Hill Reclamation Project. No, don't go out there; there's nothing to see at night. Do you know anything about the project?"

"You're trying to grow a forest in the middle of the Sahara: trees, leaf-eating molds, animals, the whole ecology." Jerryberry tried to see out through the glass. Nothing. "How's it working?"

"Well enough. If we can keep it going another thirty years, this part of the Sahara should stay a forest. Do you think we're wiping out another ecology?"

"Well, it's probably worth it here."

"The Sahara used to be a lush, green land. It was men who turned it into a desert, over thousands of years, mainly through overgrazing. We're trying to put it back."

"Okay," said Jerryberry. He heard Whyte dialing. Through the glass he could now see stars and a horizon etched with treetop shadows.

He squinted against airport-terminal lights. He asked, "How did we get through customs?"

"Oh, the Hill project is officially United States territory." Whyte swung the local directory screen out from the wall and paged through it by rapping an index finger over the touch-sensitive surface, before dialing a second time.

"Some day you'll make any journey by dialing two numbers," Whyte was saying. "Why should you have to dial your local airport first? Just dial a long-distance booth near your destination. Of course the change-over will cost us considerable. Here we are."

Bright sunlight, sandy beach, blue sea stretching to infinity. The booth was backed up against a seaside hotel. Jerryberry followed Whyte, whose careful, determined stride took him straight toward the water.

They stopped at the edge. Tiny waves brushed just to the tips of their shoes.

"Carpinteria. They advertise this beach as the safest beach in the world. It's also the dullest, of course. No waves. Remember anything about Carpinteria, Barry?"

"I don't think so."

"Oil-slick disaster. A tanker broke up out there, opposite Santa Barbara, which is up the coast a little. All of these beaches were black with oil. I was one of the volunteers working here to save the birds, to get the oil off their feathers. They died anyway."

Part of a history lesson floated to the top of Jerryberry's mind. "I thought that happened in the Gulf."

"There were many oil-related disasters. These days we ship oil by displacement booths, and we don't use anything like as much oil."

"No cars."

"No oil wells, practically."

They shifted.

From an underwater dome they gazed out at an artificial reef made from old car bodies. The shapes seemed to blend, their outlines obscured by mud and time and swarming fish. Bent and twisted metal bodies had long since rusted away, but their outlines remained, held by shellfish living and dead. Ghosts of cars, the dashboards and upholstery showing through.

The reef went on and on, disappearing into gray distance.

All those cars … Jerryberry suddenly remembered the smash-up between the El Camino and the Jaguar. The last car crash in California.

Had those cars maybe ended up here, or were they still in their collectors' proud possession? Or in that of their families?

Jerry stood and stared until Whyte hustled them off again.

"People used to joke about the East River catching fire and burning to the ground. It was that dirty," said Whyte. "Now look at it."

Things floated by: wide patches of scum, with plastic and metal objects embedded in them.

Jerryberry said, "It's pretty grubby."

"Maybe, but it's not an open sewer. Teleportation made it easier to get rid of garbage."

"I guess my trouble is I never saw anything as dirty as you claim it was. Oil slicks. Lake Michigan. The Mississippi. Maybe you're exaggerating? Just what has teleportation done for garbage collection?"

"There are records," Whyte said sternly. "Pictures."

"But even with your wonderful bottomless garbage cans, it must be easier just to dump it in the river."

Whyte fidgeted. "I guess so."

"And you still have to put the crap somewhere after you collect it."

Whyte was looking at him oddly.

"Very shrewd, Barry. Let me show you the next step."

Whyte kept his hand covered as he dialed.

"Secret," he said. "JumpShift experimental laboratory. We don't need a lot of room, because experiments with teleportation aren't particularly dangerous ..."

But there was room, lots of it. The building was a huge inflated quonset hut. Through the transparent panels Jerryberry could see other buildings, set wide apart on bare dirt. The sun was 45 degrees up. If he had known which way was north, he could have guessed longitude and latitude.

A very tall, very black woman in a lab smock greeted Whyte with glad cries. Whyte introduced her as "Gemini Jones, Ph.D."

"Gem, where do you handle disposal of radioactive waste?"

"Building Four."

The physicist's hair exploded around her head like a black dandelion. She looked down at Jerryberry with genial curiosity. "Newstaper?"

Was it that obvious? Jerryberry just nodded.

"Don't ever try to fool anyone," Jones said. "The eyes give you away."

They took the booth to Building Four. Presently they were looking down through several densities of leaded glass into a cylindrical metal chamber.

"We get a package every twenty minutes or so," said Jones. "There's a transmitter linked to this receiver in every major power plant in the United States. We keep the receiver on all the time. If a package gets reflected back, we have to find out what's wrong, and that can get hairy, because it's usually wrong at the drop-ship."

Jerryberry said, "Drop-ship?"

Gemini Jones showed surprise at his ignorance.

Whyte said, "Back up a bit, Barry. What's the most dangerous garbage ever?"

"Give me a hint."

"Radioactive wastes from nuclear power plants. Most dangerous per pound, anyway. They send those wastes here, and we send them to a drop-ship. You've got to know what a drop-ship is."

"Of course I—"

"A drop-ship is a moving teleport receiver with one end open. Generally it's attached to a space probe. The payload flicks in with a velocity different from that of the drop-ship. Of course it's supposed to come tearing out the open end, which means somebody has to keep it turned right. And of course the drop-ship only operates in vacuum."

"Package arrived," Gem Jones said softly.

Something had appeared in the metal chamber below. It was gone before Jerryberry could quite see what it was.

"Just where is your drop-ship?"

"Circling Venus," said Whyte. "Originally it was part of the second Venus expedition. You can send anything through a drop-ship: fuel, oxygen, food, water, even small vehicles. There are drop-ships circling every planet in the solar system, except Neptune.

"When the Venus expedition came home, they left the drop-ship in orbit. We thought at first that we might send another expedition through it, but—face it, Venus just isn't worth the trouble. Even if we could build enough booths and put them into the atmosphere, the atmosphere would crush and corrode the hardware within days. Maybe hours? Plus, where do we get the power to teleport away all that CO_2? So we're using the planet as a garbage dump, which is about all it's good for.

"Now, there's no theoretical reason we can't send unlimited garbage through the Venus drop-ship, as long as we keep the drop-ship oriented right. Many transmitters, one receiver. The payload doesn't stay in the receiver more than a fraction of a second. If it did get overloaded, why, some of the garbage would be reflected back to the transmitter, and we'd send it again. No problem."

"What about cost?"

"Stupendous. Horrible. Too high for any kind of garbage less dangerous than this radioactive stuff. But maybe we can bring it down someday."

Whyte stopped—he looked puzzled. "Mind if I sit down?"

There were fold-up chairs around a card table with empty soda bottles on it. Whyte sat down rather disturbingly hard, even with Gem Jones trying to support his weight.

She asked, "Can I get Doctor Janesko?"

"No, Gem, just tired. Is there more where that came from?"

Whyte was pointing at an empty bottle.

Jerryberry found the vending machine. He paid for three colas.

Turning around, he almost bumped into Gemini Jones.

She spoke low, but there was harsh intensity in her voice.

"You're running him ragged. Will you lay off of him?"

"He's been running *me*," Jerryberry whispered tersely, handing the physicist her drink.

"I believe it," she said, taking the bottle. "Well, don't let him run you so fast. Remember, he's an old man."

Jerryberry returned and put one cola on the card table.

Whyte twisted the bottle open and drank gratefully.

"Better," he sighed ... and was suddenly back in high gear.

"Now, you see, Barry? We're cleaning up the world. We aren't polluters."

"Right," Barry said, having to admit the obvious.

"Thank you."

"Now, what have you got for the mall riot?"

Whyte looked confused.

"The mall riot is still going on," Jerryberry said. "And they're still blaming me."

"And you still blame JumpShift?"

"It's a matter of access," Jerryberry said patiently. "Even if only ten men in a million, say, would loot a store, given the opportunity, that's still about four thousand people in the United States. And all four thousand can get to the Santa Monica Mall in the time it takes to dial twenty-one digits."

When Whyte spoke again, he sounded bitter.

"What are we supposed to do, stop *inventing* things?"

"No, of course not," Jerryberry said, twisting open his own cold cola.

"What, then?"

"I don't know. Just ... keep working things out."

Jerryberry drank.

"There's always another problem behind the one you just solved," Jerryberry said thoughtfully. "Does that mean you should stop solving problems? Well, let's solve this one."

They each sat in silence, sipping.

"Crowds," Jerryberry said.

"Right," was Whyte's only reply.

"You can make one receiver for many transmitters. In fact ... every booth in a city receives from any other booth. Can you make a booth that transmits only?"

Whyte looked up. "Sure. Give it an unlisted number. Potentially it would still be a receiver, of course."

"Because you have to flick the air back to the transmitter."

"How's this sound?" Whyte said, his genius brain clicking over into *solve* mode. "You can put an E on the booth number. The only dials with Es in them are at police stations and fire stations. E for Emergency."

"All right. Now, you put a lot of these escape booths wherever a crowd might gather—"

"That could be anywhere. You said so yourself."

"Yah."

"We'd have to double the number of booths in the country … or cut the number of incoming booths in half. You'd have to walk twice as far to get where you're going from any given booth. Would it be worth it?"

"I don't think this is the last riot," said Jerryberry. "It's growing. Like tourism. Your short-hop booths cut tourism way down. The long-distance booths are bringing it back, but slowly. Would you believe a permanent floating riot? A mob that travels from crowd to crowd, carrying coin purses, looting where they can."

"I hate that idea."

Jerryberry sighed and put his hand on the old man's shoulder.

"Don't worry about it," Jerryberry said, looking Whyte in the eyes. "It's my ass that's toast, not yours. You're a hero. You made a miracle. What people do with it isn't your fault. Maybe you even saved the world. The pollution was getting very rough before JumpShift came along."

"By God, it was," Whyte said fervently.

"I've got to be going," Jerryberry said. "There are still some things I want to see before I run out of time."

-8-

Tahiti. Jerusalem. Mecca. Easter Island. Stone-henge. The famous places of the world. Places a man might dial almost on impulse. Names that came unbidden to the mind.

Mecca. Vast numbers of Muslims—a number Jerryberry could look up later—bowed toward Mecca five times a day. The Koran called for every Muslim to make a pilgrimage to Mecca at least once in a lifetime. The city's only industry was the making of religious articles. And you could get there just by dialing …

Jerusalem. Sacred to three major religions. Jews still toasted each other at Passover: "Next year in Jerusalem." Still a forming ground of history after thousands of years. And a week didn't pass without the Israelis and Palestinians being in the news. And you could get there just by dialing …

Stonehenge. An ancient mystery. What race erected those stones, and when, and why? These would never be known with certainty. From the avenue at the northeast entrance a path forked and ran up a hill between burial mounds … and there was a long-distance displacement booth on the hill.

It would be eleven at night in Stonehenge. One in the morning in Mecca and Jerusalem. No action there. Jerryberry crossed them out.

Eiffel Tower, the pyramids, the Sphinx, the Vatican … dammit, the most memorable places on Earth were all in the same general area. What could Jerryberry see at midnight?

Well—*Tahiti*. Say the words, "tropical paradise," and every stranger in earshot would murmur, "Tahiti." Once Hawaii had had the same reputation, but Hawaii was too close to the world. Hawaii had been *civilized*.

Tahiti—isolated in the southern hemisphere—might have escaped that fate.

Everything lurched as Jerryberry finished dialing. He stumbled against the booth wall. Briefly, he was terrified. But he'd be dead if the velocity transfer had failed. It must be a little out of synch.

Jerryberry knew too much, now. That was all.

There were six booths of different makes this side of customs. The single official had a hopeless look. He waved through a constant stream of passengers without seeming to see them.

Jerryberry moved with the stream.

They were mostly men. Many had cameras; few had luggage. English, American, French, German, some Spanish and Russian. Most were dressed lightly—and poorly, in cheap clothes ready to come apart. They swarmed toward the outgoing booths: the rectangular Common Market booths with one glass side. Jerryberry saw unease and dismay on many faces. Perhaps it was the new, clean, modern building that bothered them.

This was an island paradise?

Air conditioning. Fluorescent lighting …

Jerryberry stood in line for the assistance desk. Then he found that it wouldn't take his coin or his credit card. On his way to the exchange counter he thought to examine the displacement booths. They took only Euros. He bought a heavy double handful of the two-color coins, then got back in line for the desk.

The computerized directory spoke English. Jerryberry used it to get a string of booth numbers in downtown Papeete.

Jerryberry was a roving newstaper again. Dial, watch the scene flick over, look around while inserting a coin, and dialing again. The coin slot was in the wrong place, but a little practice had him in the routine.

There was beachfront lined with partially built hotels in crazily original shapes. Of all the crowds Jerryberry saw in Papeete, the thickest were on the beaches and in the water. Later he could not remember the color of the sand; he hadn't seen enough of it.

Downtown he found huge blocks of buildings faced in glass, some completed, some half-built. He found old slums and old mansions. But wherever the streets ran, past mansions or slums or new skyscrapers, he found tents and lean-tos and pallet-board shacks hastily nailed together. They filled the streets, leaving small clear areas around displacement booths and public restrooms and the far-more-basic portable toilets. An open-air market ran for several blocks and was closed at both ends by crowds of tents. The only way in or out was by booth.

They're ahead, thought Jerryberry. *When you've got booths, who needs streets?*

He was not amused. He was appalled.

There were beggars. At first Jerryberry was moving too fast; he didn't realize what they were doing. But wherever he flicked in, one or two habitants immediately came toward his booth. He stopped under a vertical glass cliff of a building, where the tents of the squatters ran just to the uppermost of a flight of stone steps, and waited.

Beggars. Some were natives, men and women and children, uniform in their dark-bronze color and in their dress and their speech and the way they moved. They were a thin minority. Most were men and white and foreign. They came with their hands out, mournful or smiling; they spoke rapidly in what they guessed to be his language, and were right about half the time.

Jerryberry tried several other numbers—the beggars were *everywhere.*

Tahiti was a white man's … daydream.

Suddenly Jerryberry had had enough. On his list of jotted numbers was one that would take him out of the city. He dialed it.

Air puffed out of the booth when Jerryberry opened the door. He stretched his jaws wide—to pop his ears.

The view! He was near the peak of a granite mountain. Other mountains marched away before him, and the valleys between were green and lush. Greens and yellows and white clouds, the blue-gray of distant peaks, and beyond everything else, the sea.

It was a bus terminal. An ancient Greyhound was just pulling out. The driver stopped alongside him and shouted something amiable in French. Jerryberry smiled and shook his head violently. The driver shrugged and pulled away.

This could not have been the original terminal. Before displacement booths it could have been reached only after hours of driving. In moving the terminal up here, the touring company had saved the best for first *and* last.

The bus had looked full. Business was good.

Jerryberry stood for a long time, drinking in the view. This was the beauty that had made Tahiti famous. It was good to know that Tahiti's population explosion had left something intact.

Presently, Jerryberry remembered he was running on a time limit. He walked around to the ticket window.

The young man in the booth laid a paperback book face down. He smiled agreeably. "Yes?"

"Do you speak English?"

"Certainly." He wore a kind of uniform, but his features and color were those of a Tahitian. His English was good, the accent not quite French. "Would you like to buy a tour ticket?"

"No, thanks. I'd like to talk, if you have a minute."

"What would you like to talk about?"

"Tahiti. I'm a newstaper."

The man's smile drooped a bit. "And you wish to give us free publicity."

"Something like that."

The smile was gone. "You may return to your country and tell them that Tahiti is full."

"I noticed that. I have just come from Papeete."

"I have the honor to own a house in Papeete, a good property. We, my family and myself, we have been forced to move out! There was no—no *paysage*"—he was too angry to talk as fast as he wanted—"no passage from the house to anyplace. We were surrounded by the tents of the"—he used a word Jerryberry did not recognize—"and we could not buy an instant motion booth for the house. I had not the money. We could not have moved the booth to the house because the"—that word again—"blocked the streets. The police can do nothing. Nothing!"

"Why not?"

"There are too many. We are not monsters; we cannot simply shoot them. It would be the only way to stop them. They come without money or clothing or any place to stay. And they are not the worst. You will tell people this when you return?"

"I'm recording," said Jerryberry.

"Tell them that the worst are those with *much* money, those who build hotels. They would turn our island into an enormous hotel! See!"

The man pointed where Jerryberry could not have seen himself, down the slope of the mountain. "Hilton, Ramada, Marriott, it doesn't matter, they all come and they all buy and they all build, build, *build*."

Jerryberry looked down to temporary buildings and a great steel box with helicopter rotors on it. He filmed it on the digital Minox, then filmed a panoramic sweep of the mountains beyond, and finished with the scowling man in the ticket booth.

"*Squatters*," the ticket-taker said suddenly. "The English word I wanted. The squatters are in my house now, I am sure of it, in my house since we moved out. Tell the world we want no more *squatters*!"

"I'll tell them," said Jerryberry.

Before he left, Jerryberry took one more long look about him. Green valleys, gray-blue mountains, distant line of sea … but his eyes kept dropping to the endless stream of supplies that poured from the cargo booth that was servicing the hotel construction site below.

Easter Island. Tremendous, long-faced, solemn stone statues with topknots of red volcanic tuff. Cartoons of the statues were even more common than pictures. ("Shut up until those archaeologists leave," one statue whispers to another.) And even pictures can only hint at the statues' massive solemnity. But you could get there just by dialing …

Except that the directory wouldn't give Jerryberry a booth number for Easter Island.

Surely there must be booth travel to Easter Island. Mustn't there? But how eager would the Peruvian government be to see a million tourists on Easter Island?

Ah. The other side of the coin. Displacement booths made any place infinitely accessible, but only if you moved a booth in.

Jerryberry was grinning with delight as he dialed Los Angeles International.

There was a defense!

-9-

AT THE POLICE STATION on Purdue Avenue, Jerryberry couldn't get anyone to talk to him. But the patience of a newstaper is unique in a world of instant transportation. He kept at it.

Eventually a deskman stopped long enough to tell him, "Look, we don't have time. Everybody's out cleaning up the mall riot."

"Cleaning up? Is it over?"

"Just about. We had to move in old riot vehicles from Chicago. I guess we'll have to start building them again. But it's over."

"Good!"

"Too right. I don't mean to say we got them all. Some looters managed to jury-rig a cargo booth in the basement of that damned department store. They moved their loot out that way and then got out that way themselves. We're going to hate it the next time they show up. They've got guns now."

"A permanent, floating riot?"

"Something like that. Look, I don't have time to talk." And he was back on the phone.

The next man Jerryberry stopped recognized him at once. "You're the man who started it all! Will you get out of my way?"

90

Jerryberry left, his face gone both pink and hot.

Sunset on a summer evening. It was cocktail hour again … three and a half hours later.

Jerryberry felt unaccountably dizzy outside the police station. He rested against the wall.

Too much change. Over and over again he had shifted place and time and climate. From evening in New York to a humid seacoast to the dry furnace of Death Valley to night in the Sahara. It was hard to remember where he was. He had lost direction.

When he felt better, Jerryberry shifted to the Cave des Roys.

For each human being there is an optimum ratio between change and stasis. Too little change, he grows bored. Too little stability, he panics and loses his ability to adapt. One who marries six times in ten years will not change jobs. One who moves often to serve his company will maintain a stable marriage. A woman chained to one home and family may redecorate frantically or take a lover or go to many costume parties.

Displacement booths make novelty easy. Stability comes hard. For many, the clubs were an element of stability. A lot of the key clubs were chains; a man could leave his home in Wyoming and find his club again in Denver. Members tended to resemble one another. A man changing roles would change clubs.

Clubs were places to meet people, as buses and airports and even neighborhoods no longer were. Some clubs were good for pickups ("This card gets me laid!") while others were for heavy conversation.

At the Beach Club you could always find a paddle-tennis game.

The Cave was for quiet and stability.

A quick drink and the cool darkness of the Cave's bar were just what Jerryberry needed. He looked into the lights in the wall of bottles and tried to remember a name. When it came, he jotted it down, then finished his drink at leisure.

Harry McCord had been police chief in Los Angeles for twelve years and had been on the force for far longer. He had retired only last year. The computer directory took some time to find him. He was living on the coast in Lincoln City, Oregon.

Harry had a small house in the middle of a pine forest just up off the beach. From McCord's back porch Jerryberry could see the gravel path that circled lazily down to the sand.

Harry offered his guest a tallboy. They drank beer while sitting in Adirondack chairs.

"Crime is a pretty general subject," said Harry McCord.

"Crime and displacement booths," said Jerryberry. "I want to know how your job was affected by the instant getaway."

Jerryberry waited.

"Pretty drastically, I guess. The booths came in, but they came slowly. We had a chance to get used to them. Let's see; there were people who put displacement booths in their living rooms, and when they got robbed, they blamed us."

McCord talked haltingly at first, then gaining speed. He had always been something of a public figure. He talked well.

Burglary: The honors were even there. If the house or apartment had an alarm, the police could be on the scene almost instantly. If the burglar moved fast enough to get away, he certainly wouldn't have time to rob his target.

There were sophisticated alarms now that would lock the displacement booth door from the inside. Often that held the burglar up just long enough for the police to shift in. At opposite extremes of professionalism, there were men who could get through an alarm system without setting it off—in which case there wasn't a hope in hell of catching them after they'd left—and men who had been caught robbing apartment houses because they'd forgotten to take coins for the booth in the lobby.

"Then there was Lon Willis," Harry said. "His MO was to prop the booth door open before he went to work on the house. If he set the alarm off, he'd run next door and use that booth. Worked pretty well—it slowed us up just enough that we never did catch him. But one night he set off an alarm, and when he ran next door, the next-door neighbor blew a small but adequate hole in him."

Murder: The alibi was an extinct species. A man attending a party in Hawaii could shoot a man in Paris in the time it would take him to use the bathroom. "Like George Clayton Larkin did. Except that he used his credit card, and we got him," said McCord. "Never use your credit card. And we got Lucille Downey because she ran out of coins and had to ask at the magazine stand for change. With blood all over her sleeves!"

Pickpockets ...

"Do you have a lock pocket?" McCord asked.

"Sure," said Jerryberry. It was an inside pocket lined with tough plastic. The zipper lock took two hands to open. "They're tough to get into, but not impossible."

"What's in it? Credit and debit cards?"

"Right."

"And you can cancel them in three minutes. Picking pockets isn't profitable anymore. If it was, they would have mobbed the mall riot."

Smuggling: nobody even tried to stop it.

Drugs: "There's no way to keep people from getting them. And that was true even before the booths. Anyone who wants drugs can get drugs. We made arrests where we could, and so what? Me, I'm betting on Darwin."

"How do you mean?"

"The next generation won't use drugs because they'll be descended from people who had better sense. I'd legalize wireheading if it were up to me. With a wire in your pleasure center, you're getting what all the drugs are supposed to give you, and no dope peddler can hold out on you."

Riots: The mall riot was the first successful riot in twenty years.

"The police can get to a riot before it's a riot," said McCord. "We call them flash crowds, and we watch for them. We've been doing it ever since … well, ever since it became possible."

He hesitated and evidently decided to go on. "See, the coin booths usually went into the shopping centers first and then the residential areas. It wasn't till JumpShift put them in the slum areas that we stopped having riots."

"Makes sense," Jerryberry said.

McCord laughed. "Even that's a half-truth. When the booths went into the slums, we pretty near stopped having slums. Everyone moved out. They'd commute."

"Why do you think the police didn't stop the mall riot?"

"That's a funny one, isn't it? I was there this afternoon. Did you get a chance to look at the perps' cargo booth in the department store's basement? It's a professional job. Whoever rigged it knew exactly what he was doing. No slips. He probably had a model to practice on. We traced it to a cargo receiver in downtown L.A., but we don't know where it was sending to, because someone stayed behind and wrecked it and then shifted out. Real professional. Some gang has decided to make a profession of riots."

"You think this is their first job?"

"I'd guess, but they planned extensively. They must have seen the mall-type riots coming. Theoretical. Which is pretty shrewd, because a flash crowd couldn't have formed that fast before long-distance displacement booths. It's a new crime. Makes me almost sorry I retired."

"How would you redesign the booths to make life easier for the police?"

But McCord wouldn't touch the subject. He didn't know anything about booth design.

Seven o'clock. The interview with Wash Evans was at ten.

Jerryberry shifted back to the Cave. He was beginning to get nervous. The Cave, and a good dinner, should help ease his stage fright.

He turned down a couple of invitations to join small groups. With the interview hanging over his head, he'd be poor company. He sat alone and continued to jot during dinner.

Escape booths. Send anywhere, receive only from police and fire departments.

Police can shut down all booths in an area. Except escape booths? No, that would let looters escape, too. But there might be no way to stop that. At least it would get innocent bystanders out of a riot area.

Hah! Escape booths send only to police station!

Jerryberry blanked that out and wrote, *All booths send only to police stations!*

He blanked that out, too, to write an expanded version:

1. Riot signal from police station.

2. All booths in area stop receiving.

3. All booths in area send only to police station.

Jerryberry went back to eating. Moments later he stopped with his fork half raised, put it down, and wrote:

4. A million rioters stomp police station to rubble, from inside.

Jerryberry sighed. It had seemed like such a good idea.

He was dawdling over coffee when the rest of it dropped into place.

Jerryberry went to a phone.

The secretary at Seven Sixes promised to have Dr. Whyte call as soon as he checked in. Jerryberry put a time limit on it, which seemed to please her.

McCord wasn't home.

Jerryberry went back to his coffee. He was feeling twitchy now. He had to know if this was possible. Otherwise he would be talking out his ass—and in front of a big audience, too.

Twenty minutes later, as Jerryberry was about to call again, an unlisted number began buzzing his cell phone.

"It's a design problem," said Jerryberry. "Let me tell you how I'd like it to work, and then you can tell me if it's possible, okay?"

"Go ahead."

"First step is the police get word of a flash crowd, a mall riot-type crowd. They throw emergency switches at headquarters. Each switch affects the displacement booths in a small area."

"That's the way it works now."

"Now those switches turn off the booths. I'd like them to do something more complex. Set them so they can only receive from police and fire departments and can only transmit to a police station."

"We can do that. Good. Then the police could release the innocent bystanders, send the injured to a hospital, hold the obvious looters, get everybody's names … right. Brilliant. You'd put the receiver at the top of a greased slide, and have a *big* cell at the bottom."

"Maybe. At least the receiver would be behind bars."

"You could issue override cards to the police and other authorities to let them shift in through a blockade."

"Good."

Whyte's voice stopped suddenly. "There's a hole in it. A really big crowd would either wreck the station, or smother—depending on how strong the cell was. Did you think of that?"

"I'd like to use more than one police station," Jerryberry said.

"How many? There's a distance limit. Barry, what are you thinking?"

"As it stands now, a long-distance passenger has to dial three numbers to get anywhere. You said you could cut that to two. Can you cut it to one?"

"I don't know."

"It's poetic justice," said Jerryberry. "Our whole problem is that rioters can converge on one point from all over the United States. If we could use police stations all over the United

States, we wouldn't have a problem. As soon as a cell was full here, we'd switch to police stations in San Diego or Tacoma!"

Whyte was laughing.

"You can't do it," Jerryberry said, deflated.

"No, of course we can't do it. Wait … wait just a damned minute."

Whyte took a deep breath.

"There's a way," Whyte said. "We could do it if there was a long-distance receiver at the police station. Hook the network to a velocity damper. I told you, there's no reason you shouldn't be able to dial to a long-distance receiver from any booth."

"It would work?"

"You'd have to talk the public into paying for it. Design wouldn't be much of a problem. We could cover the country with an emergency network in a couple of years."

"Can I quote you?"

"Of course. We sell displacement booths. That's our business."

-10-

TALK SHOWS WERE ONE OF THE FEW remaining pure entertainment features on television. With DVDs the viewer bought a static package; with a talk show she never knew just what she would be getting. It was a different product. It was cheap to produce. It could compete with the reality TV junk.

The Tonight Show aired at 8:30 P.M., prime time.

Around nine they started flicking in, pouring out of the booths that lined the street above the last row of houses. They milled about, searching out the narrow walks that led down to the strand. They poured over the low stone wall that guarded the sand from the houses.

They paused, awed.

Breakers rolled in from the black sea, flashing electric-blue.

Within minutes Hermosa Beach was swarming with people: men, women, children—in couples and family groups. They held hands and looked out to sea. They stamped the packed wet sand, dancing like savages, and whooped with delight to see blue light flash beneath their feet. High up on the dry sand were piles of discarded clothing. Swimmers were thick in the water, splashing blue fire at each other.

Many were drunk, or high on this or that, when *The Tonight Show* led them there. Those who came were happy to start with. They came to do a happy thing. Some carried six-packs or pouches of marijuana.

The line of them stretched around the curve of the shore to the north, beyond Hermosa Pier to the south, bunching around the pier. More were shifting in all the time, trickling down to join the others.

Jerryberry flicked in almost an hour early for the interview.

The station was an ant's nest: a swarm of furious disorganization.

Jerryberry was looking for Wash Evans when Wash Evans came running past him from behind, glanced back, and stopped to a jarring halt.

"Hi," said Jerryberry. "Is there anything we need to go over before we go on?"

Evans seemed at a loss. "Yah," he said, and caught his breath a little.

"You're not news anymore, Jansen. We may not even be doing the interview."

Jerryberry cursed. "I heard they'd cleared up the riot—"

"More than that. They caught the lady shoplifter."

"Good," Jerryberry said honestly.

"If you say so. One out of a thousand people that recognized your pictures of her turned out to be right. Woman by the name of Irma Hennessey, lives in Jersey City but commutes all over the country. She says she's never hit the same store twice. She's a kick, Jansen. A newstaper's dream. No offense intended, but I wish they'd let her out of jail tonight. I'd interview her."

"So I didn't cause the mall riot anymore, now you've got Irma Hennessey. Well, good. I didn't like being a celebrity. Anything else?"

Evans said, "Yah, there's a new riot going on at Hermosa Beach."

"What the hell?"

"Craziest damn thing. You know Gordon Lundt, the movie star? He was on *The Tonight Show*, and he happened to mention the red tide down at Hermosa Beach. He said it was pretty. The next thing anyone knows, every man, woman, and child in the country has decided he wants to see the red tide at Hermosa Beach."

"How bad is it?"

"Well, nobody's been hurt, last I heard. And they aren't breaking things. It's not that kind of crowd, and there's nothing to steal but sand, anyway. It's a happy riot, Jansen. There's just a fuckload of a lot of people."

"Another flash crowd. It figures," said Jerryberry. "You can get a flash crowd anywhere there are displacement booths."

"Can you?"

"Sudden mobs have been around a long time. It's just that they happen faster with the long-distance booths. Some places are permanent floating flash crowds. Like Tahiti ... what's wrong?"

Wash Evans had a funny look. "It just hit me that we don't really have anything to replace you with. You've been doing your homework, have you?"

"All day." Jerryberry dug out the Minox. "I've been everywhere I could think of. Some of this goes with interviews." He produced the digital audio recorder. "Of course there isn't much time to sort it out—"

"No. Gimme." Evans took the camera and the recorder. "We can follow up on these later. Maybe they'll make a special. Right now the news is at Hermosa Beach. And you sound like you know how it happened and what to do about it. Do you still want to do that interview?"

"I—sure."

"Go get a C.B.A. camera from George Bailey. Let's see, it's—nine fifteen, dammit. Spend half an hour, see as much as you can, then get back here. Find out what you can about the flash crowd at Hermosa Beach. That's what we'll be talking about."

George Bailey looked up as Jerryberry arrived. He pointed emphatically at the single camera remaining on the table, finger-combed the hair back out of his eyes, and went back to monitoring half a dozen screens.

The gyroscopically mounted smooth-pan digital camera came satisfyingly to life in Jerryberry's hands. He picked up a list of Hermosa Beach numbers and turned to the displacement booths. Too much coffee sloshed in his belly. He stopped suddenly, thinking.

One big riot-control center would do it. You wouldn't need a police network. Just one long-distance receiver to serve the whole country, and a building the size of a football stadium. Or bigger? Big enough to handle *any* riot. A federal police force on permanent guard. Rioting was an interstate crime now anyway. You could build such a center faster and cheaper than any network.

Jerryberry filed the idea for his discussion with Wash.

Now, back to work.

He stepped into a booth, dialed, and was gone.

Wash hadn't been kidding. Hermosa was a zoo.

But not in the way the mall had been a zoo.

People were, for the most part, friendly. Jammed shoulder to shoulder. But friendly. Little knots formed here and there as different visitors discovered fellow travelers from the same city, or the same town, or the same state. Like old home week. They meandered together slowly down to the sand, and experienced the magic of the red tide—glowing eerie blue in the night. Then they moved back up the beach and headed for home. Wherever home happened to be.

This time, law enforcement was trying to get out ahead of potential problems. There were enough uniformed police sprinkled throughout the mass of people that anyone with funny ideas thought better of it.

Jerryberry caught footage of the whole thing, adding his own commentary along the way. Occasionally someone recognized him—once they got up close enough to see who he was in the dim light—but now Jerryberry didn't feel so sheepish. The heat seemed to be off. He wasn't the goat anymore. The stain of infamy had been mostly removed.

"Barry!" a woman's voice said loudly over the din of the crowd.

Jerryberry stopped recording, and waited while someone pushed her way through the people and reached him.

Janice Wolfe was wearing a flattering one-piece swimsuit and flip-flop sandals that slapped her heels as she walked.

"I can't believe you saw me in all these faces—and in the dark, too!" Jerryberry practically yelled to her over the noise of the crowd.

"When I saw the little LED lights from the camera weaving around in the throng, I was curious to find out if it was you. Come for the red tide, or for the people-watching?"

"A little of both. C.B.A. still wants my interview, with additional coverage on what's happening here. For contrast. Violent riots versus quiet riots, I guess?"

"That's good, right?" Janice said.

"Yes," Jerryberry said.

"You look exhausted," Janice said when she got up close to him, her body pressed against his side. *A not unpleasant sensation,* Jerryberry thought silently. The smash of people didn't give either one of them a lot of room in which to maneuver.

"Quite," Jerryberry said. "But if I was feeling mildly apocalyptic this morning, things look a lot better now. Thanks again for being a sounding board when I needed it, Janice."

"What are friends for?" she said, smiling.

"Well, I'm about done here," Jerryberry said. "You going to go in and take a swim?"

"I thought about it," Janice said, wrinkling her nose. "But with all those people in the water, it's bound to be a soup by now."

"Janice, it started that way. Red plankton soup. You'd need a shower."

"Yeah? I'll pass."

"You going to watch my live interview with Wash? I'm going to be making a rather out-of-the-box proposal to the people of the United States."

"Do tell? Yes, I'll watch. About Evans, do you think he'll play the part of friend, or foe?"

"With Wash, it'll be a little bit of both. But I'm ready for him this time. You won't believe who I've been talking to today. Together we figured out how to beat riots. Forever."

"Do tell?"

"Maybe I'll give you the full story when the Evans interview is over. Up for a late-night snack when I get home?"

"Absolutely," Janice said, and leaned in to give Jerryberry a peck on the cheek.

Then she was gone, moving back into the crowd from whence she had come.

Jerryberry stood there dumbly, his hand absently rubbing the place on his face where her warm lips had touched his skin.

Then he smiled, wrapped up his equipment, and pushed determinedly for the nearest booth.

BOOK TWO:
DIAL AT RANDOM

LARRY NIVEN

Robin Whyte was approaching a booth when a naked man and woman flicked in front of him. They were wrapped around each other, but grinning out of the booth at any passersby. Robin froze for a second. Then his sense of humor kicked in, and he opened the door, interrupting their progress.

The booth was narrow, but they were both small and lean. They were standing on their luggage, one bag each. They barely fit. Robin remembered, from years ago, a misty gray view of the interiors of a pair of lean Dutch scientists having sex in an MRI machine.

The man shouted. "Close the door!"

She talked over him, smiling brilliantly. "Hi! We just got married."

He said, "Come on, close the door. We're flicking down Ventura Boulevard—"

Robin Whyte asked, "Trying to set a record for streaking?"

"Yeah, and you're interfering! Close the door!"

Robin looked around. Murphy's Law held: there was a cop approaching on a Segway. Ventura Boulevard was clogged with pedestrians going to work this early morning, but those nearby had stopped to look. The cop was weaving among them, coming fast.

There should still be time. Robin Whyte pulled out a calling card, flipped it inside and closed the door. The pair flicked out. Robin opened the booth, stepped in and inserted his jump card into the Pay slot. He tapped at the destination keyboard: Home 4 Go, three symbols that flicked him out.

He was grinning. The couple should be easy to track. They'd been in Meander mode, taking three seconds each to flick from booth to booth, giving them a changing panoramic view. They must have acquired something like a Press jump card. Transit mode was faster, but not too fast: you still had to absorb kinetic or potential energy differences. Long Range was still experimental, but that was what Robin was using.

And Robin had already arrived outside Home 4, the JumpShift factory in the Mojave Desert. It was nearly nine in the morning.

Home 4 was Lightspeed Labs, which made and tested experimental teleportation gear.

One of the first lessons they'd learned at JumpShift Inc. was: don't put the booth inside your home. You make it too easy for burglars. Robin had to go through Security just like everyone else. A generic-looking white man in his forties, he was dressed to face the public: grey suit, pink turtleneck, clean-shaven, a sheer white smile. He asked the guard, "How's it going?"

"Lots of people coming in, ever since six. You're one of the latest, Mr. Whyte."

The weather was fine. Not too much wind. Not that that mattered here; Hosni would be making his own wind. Robin went on in.

The factory floor was big. Thirty people didn't crowd it. Most were JumpShift employees. Eight or ten were labeled PRESS; they were manipulating video cameras, or trying to talk to Hosni, or videotaping a quite ordinary JumpShift booth and the big circuit board beside it, which weren't doing anything. Action centered around a weirdly garbed Hosni Lasalle. Hosni was thoroughly padded, wearing a hardshelled pressure suit and a parachute. The aeroshell stood nearby, open, but looking like a heavily streamlined man.

The helmet was tipped back from Hosni's head. He spotted Robin and raised a thumb (all's okay) while continuing to talk to a pretty woman in her thirties. Robin didn't interrupt.

It was early days for JumpShift Inc. Robin Whyte was in the business of selling teleportation. It would be a lot easier if you could teleport anywhere with the flick of a credit card, and JumpShift's publicity was likely to leave that impression. And you *could* do that. It was just that, flicking around on the surface of a spinning ball, you had to face certain laws of physics.

The conservation laws held. Flick a mile uphill and you gained potential energy and dropped some real energy: a temperature drop of seven degrees Fahrenheit if you were made of, say, water. Teleport west and you'd be driven into the ground: bend your knees as if you were using a parachute. East, you'd be lifted off your feet. South or north, you'd be shoved sideways. A little of that was no worse than driving a car over speed bumps, or around a turn, if you weren't flicking very far. Or you could take several jumps in a row: Transit mode.

The trick, for JumpShift, was to sell as many booths as possible while looking for a way to compensate for the conservation laws. If you didn't sell enough booths … it would be like the electric cars of Robin's childhood. If you didn't have plugs in enough gas stations, you'd be stranded over and over. Why not buy a gas guzzler instead?

There were people who really ought to have instant transportation. Robin had booths in the Kremlin, the White House, a score of seats of government, a few embassies. Altogether he'd sold about sixty thousand booths. Not bad. And if the new system worked, JumpShift would be more popular than ever.

Robin maintained his business smile while he talked to various employees. This publicity stunt could make the difference between success and bankruptcy. Because, yes, you could flick a quarter of the way around a spinning globe, if that was what you wanted. You just had to be ready for the consequences.

If he'd done this closer to the Equator—but Hosni was taking enough risk. Robin looked at screens set around the cafeteria. There were cameras all over *Moby Dick*, the yacht (leased) floating ninety miles offshore from Spain. Hosni's lateral velocity at the Mojave Desert end would become vertical, straight up from the ocean surface, as he left the spit cage aboard *Moby Dick*. The aeroshell was there because he'd be going supersonic.

Twenty years ago, a man in a pressure suit had stepped out of a balloon floating at stratospheric heights. He'd cracked supersonic speed on the way down, and become famous forever. Hosni would be falling supersonic in both directions.

And it was time. Robin stepped forward to shake hands with the test pilot and wish him luck, a videotape moment. With a couple of assistants Hosni sealed himself into the aeroshell. Cameras everywhere: good. Robin could picture fools claiming that the shell was empty when it left *Moby Dick*. Now Hosni was carried toward a booth just like sixty thousand others scattered around the world, except for the bank of controls next to it.

And now there was a girl in the booth. The men carrying Hosni froze.

Mid-teens, white, pretty, dressed for a party, looking around her like most travelers just flicking into a booth. She was holding a jump card.

Robin Whyte could not remember moving faster. The instrument wall was four steps away. Robin lunged past a staring assistant and flicked the power off aboard *Moby Dick*'s spit cage. The signal would take four one-hundredths of a second to reach the ship.

The girl looked around her, puzzled, then annoyed. She slid the jump card into its slot, which somebody should damned well have disabled, and was gone without typing a destination.

***

The Farmer's Market had spilled outward into 3rd Street and Fairfax. Shops formed barriers that forced what remained of traffic into curved paths and obstacle courses. The bicyclists and rollerboarders seemed to like it that way. There was just space for trams and carts to deliver goods from the JumpShift booths.

Hilary Firestone flicked into a booth set in the newer section. She stepped out onto concrete and fading white and yellow lines. It was just past seven in the morning, and the summer sun was halfway up the sky.

The Farmer's Market was ninety years old, though most of the shops were not. These shops spread across the hot pavement did not have a makeshift look; they had been there for years. One sold scores of varieties of candles. One sold tobacco, pot, bongs and pipes. Several sold fruits and vegetables. One sold chickens and eggs, and another was a butcher shop—but those were above the curb, in the older section, where cars had parked before the coming of the JumpShift booths.

Hilary was fourteen years old, tall, with straight black hair and skin too white to take a suntan. She was dressed for last night's party, in white jeans and a scarlet blouse with a cartoon video playing across it, Coyote in hot pursuit of Roadrunner, around and around. A small leather purse hung on a strap over her shoulder. A minute ago she'd been in the mountains above Malibu. She looked around, a girl in a hurry—but breakfast was looking at her, a fruit stand that displayed orange juice squeezed before your eyes. She bought a large cup and gulped it as she walked. Here was coffee, here were breads, here were tables not yet occupied. Anything she wanted.

Her parents had expected her to do this shopping yesterday evening. They were planning to come home tonight, but you couldn't count on that, given JumpShift technology. Forget something? Pills, reading glasses, need a bathroom? Just flick home for a minute. And where's Hilary?

Breakfast finished, Hilary began her run. What did she need? Double-roasted peanuts. Pecan pralines. Groceries: a cut-up chicken, asparagus, some eggs and a container of egg yolks: maybe Mom would make hollandaise. Buy a couple of eccentrically shaped candles, they might make good gifts. Skim through that bookstore. The key here was to get home before her parents did, with enough of what she'd come for to show some serious shopping. It didn't much matter what she bought. Just enough to cover for last night's party.

With her arms full of bags she stepped into 3rd Street and fumbled out her jump card.

It looked like a credit card: rectangular, with a magnetic strip. During Hilary's year as a freshman at the Cate boarding school, that card had lived in the Headmaster's safe. Her parents did not fully trust their only daughter. Maybe these restrictions were the reason some friends called her "Hilarity": she was sullen too often; she never got to do anything. There were approved addresses on the card. Emergency stuff: police, fire, hospital, the family lawyer. Cate School. Family and family friends. Addresses were added when Dad approved: a coffee shop, girl friends, yoga class, the Farmer's Market. From anywhere not on the card, the card would take her straight home.

The booth looked like one end of a test tube: round and made of hardened glass, with a rounded top. It was big enough for two, or for one and some luggage. Hilary stepped toward the booth, fumbled a paper bag, regained her balance and dropped the card. She stooped to reach for it without setting anything down.

A tall boy on inline skates came out from behind a candy stand. Two more behind him. She glimpsed him coming, shied back and fell on her butt, spilling groceries but ducking a collision. The kid ran over her jump card, leaning way out to touch her hair as he passed. They all kept going, laughing like maniacs.

Breathing hard, Hilary picked up the card. It was bent.

Even as she wailed in fury, she thought: maybe, maybe there was a nugget of good news in this disaster.

Darrell Tooney had already fiddled with her card. He'd added his own address, the locus of last night's party in Malibu. If the card was ruined, Dad would never find the added locus ... the address of a boy Dad didn't know. On the other hand, how was she going to get home? Well, maybe she'd ask a shopkeeper for help.

But first: bend the card back into shape. There, that didn't look bad. Now try the card.

Hilary picked up her bags and retrieved spilled groceries. She stepped into the booth, closed the door, inserted the card below the keypad. The system swallowed it. She was about to type in HOME when the booth triggered and flicked her away.

She was expecting a series of jumps. The way it usually went, each booth sent you to the next within reach in the direction you wanted to go. You'd get flick flick flick, bump bump bump as you absorbed the kinetic energy. If the jump was too far, the card popped out and left you—wherever.

But she'd flicked only once. Hilary *knew* that home wasn't that close.

The light had changed: the sun had dropped. As she stepped out she smelled ocean. Where was she?

Not in Brentwood, that was sure. She was looking down toward scores of people, all lined up along a shoreline, every one of them facing away from her, shifting as they stared at ... what?

Of course she could step back into the booth. But there was something wrong with her jump card. No telling where it would take her. But what *were* they looking at?

She set the groceries down outside the booth. Forcing her way through that crowd ... might have been possible, but she saw something better. She saw a tree.

Hilary was good at climbing trees. Big branches were low to the ground. In moments she was above the crowd, looking through branches, above the tops of their heads, at blue horizon and below that ... ohmyGod. Whales!

Had to be whales. Too big to be seals. She was seeing mostly curls of white water, but black shapes surfacing within, and wow. She'd heard tales of whales from a cousin who'd been in the San Juan Islands, a thousand miles north of Brentwood.

The whales were tracking to the right ... had to be north if that was the Pacific. Hilary watched while most of an hour passed. Presently she climbed down, thinking hard.

Broken card. Could take her anywhere. Why wasn't she feeling the bumps? Or she could stroll on down to the shore and ask for help. Some stranger would escort her home. No danger, not with so many witnesses. Or she could phone her parents.

Could take her anywhere. She'd never have a chance like this again.

The scene jumped, and suddenly Hilary was surrounded by videocameras and people all watching her through the booth wall.

Four men were carrying a man in a transparent shell. They stopped moving when they saw her; the man in the shell yelped and tried to tell her something. An older man jerked like a marionette, then lunged for a big control board.

For an instant Hilary was tempted to do something weird. Flash them, maybe. But she could already be in trouble. Her ruined jump card might serve as an excuse for anything ... maybe.

Maybe not. Better get out. Hilary inserted her card into the PAY slot and was gone.

The others were still reacting. Robin Whyte was watching the screens. *Moby Dick*'s deck was clear around the spit cage.

Spit cages were still somewhat experimental. If this worked ... despite its makeshift look, it was a JumpShift booth open at one end. Velocities wouldn't matter if you aimed it right. If a cargo came through from the Mojave, it would flash straight up through the throat of the spit cage and into the sky at twice sonic speed. And if that cargo was a teenage girl protected by nothing more than an active-view T shirt, Robin would see a fireball. She'd be torn to bits and burnt to ash.

But nothing was going through. He'd turned the link off in time.

The girl was certainly gone. She might have been no more than a hallucination.

Robin flicked the switch that would restore power to *Moby Dick*. Power flow … dials … spit cage status … all looked good. Robin picked a technician whose name he knew and tapped his shoulder. "Check me out, Wade," he said. "Is this nominal?"

Wade Hench stared. "You're sending him through?"

"I don't see a problem."

"The girl?"

"We'll have to deal with that." Robin stepped to a microphone. "Break for fifteen minutes," he said. He motioned to the four men holding Hosni in his glass shell. "Hosni? Fifteen minutes, then go."

Cameras had caught the girl. Readings had caught her arrival, and another signature: a wave of energy to a mass in Lake Mead. The link that could make JumpShift a long distance proposition was working, and some unnamed girl was using it.

Fifteen minutes later they rolled Hosni into the booth. Robin himself flicked the switch that flicked him out.

Hilary stepped out onto a lawn, and stepped around a stone marker. The sun was high, noonish. Rows and rows of stone markers, and a densely packed crowd being well dressed and very politely quiet, just a few people whispering. An oddly dressed man at the front was speaking of … well, of a very accomplished woman who must be dead, because this was a cemetery. Cameras were panning over the crowd. She heard a name, "Miranda Troost," and recognized it from school: the Secretary of State, dead of a stroke.

How in Hell could she have reached Washington, DC?

Hilary looked straight into a camera, then decided this wasn't the fun she had anticipated. For an instant she considered: she could wait around and ask for help from a gravedigger. Instead, she returned to the booth and her bags and flicked out.

It was cold. She was in cramped rectangular space, under dim lights. The booth was pushed into one end of a corridor.

That alone was strange. A booth in your living space was an invitation to home invasion. People didn't usually install JumpShift booths inside. Hilary stepped out to see more. She called, "Hello?"

The air was musty. The corridor was padded with something like cork, perhaps for soundproofing. It led to a solid-looking door, also padded. She opened it and found another door. It was colder yet, and this looked like an airlock. She couldn't imagine that she was on the Moon—JumpShift booths wouldn't do *that*—but where was she?

Nobody had answered her hail.

She closed the first door, the inner door. Half-expecting vacuum, half-compelled by curiosity, Hilary wrestled the outer door open. A terrible freezing wind fought her, and then she was out.

She was in a glare of horizontal sunlight. Pinpoints of dry snow stung her skin. Everywhere about her was ice. Dirty ice formed paths. Paths circled a tall pole sticking out of the ice. One path led from the pole to here. A wide loop around the pole led to a little hut that looked like wood ... Lord, that was a sauna, she thought. Hilary recognized this place from pictures and an article in National Geographic.

But how could she be here? Teleport booths wouldn't send this far, not without killing you.

Shapes burst from the hut: naked men moving at a run, a file of six. Their arms half-hid their eyes, protecting. They ran straight at the pole. There was a big box on top of the pole, and it was moving to follow the men. A videotape camera.

She'd been right: this was the three hundred degree run. From two hundred degrees Fahrenheit in the sauna, into minus one hundred as you ran naked to circle the North Pole.

Did they have a setup like this at the South Pole too? But this had to be the North Pole because the sun was up, because it was northern hemisphere summer. The first man slapped the pole, took the turn and saw Hilary. He kept running. It was the fourth man who stopped, staring, letting the others pass him.

Hilary stood gaping. The man stared back … then ran for the sauna.

Hilary crouched, wrapped arms around her head, and wobbled backward into the airlock. No wonder they didn't lock it. Lock a person out and she'd be frozen dead.

She stared at the jump card before she used it again. Conservation of energy had consequences. Flick north or south, velocity change from the Earth's spin would kick you sideways; flick east or west, you'd be lifted or slammed down. Flick a mile uphill, you'd lose heat energy. Downhill, you could faint from heat exhaustion.

Her card certainly hadn't been tagged to send her to the North Pole, before that idiot bent it. The card was jumping her at random.

She didn't really have a problem, she decided. As soon as she flicked into a residential zone, she'd ask for help. Anyway, what choice did she have? Face down half a dozen naked men? Dad would freak. She stepped into the booth and inserted the damaged card.

It was night. Burning torches didn't give much more light than the full moon.

The houses were made of cloth: elaborate tents in various muted shades, brown and gray. She couldn't guess where she was. She was surrounded by black-skinned children and adults, none of them moving very much. Lots of children. They looked at her through the glass. Lean arms and legs: they looked more than half starved.

Hilary opened the jump booth. She pushed one of her grocery bags outside. She closed the door and flicked out.

The sun was in the right place. Maybe she'd gotten lucky. But the floor wobbled and she knew she was on a boat. A twenty-foot motorboat, looked like, with a booth and pile of batteries in the middle.

Other boats seemed to be arrayed around her. One was an ambulance ship with a red cross on it. One, a Coast Guard cruiser. The horizon was water in all directions, and a brilliant sun right at the edge. She'd gone back to dawn.

Hilary stayed in the booth until she saw, in the sky above the ocean, something she recognized. One of the Goodyear blimps. Spanish words scrolled across its flank in brilliant electric light. Then English: JUMPSHIFT INTRODUCES HOSNI LASALLE IN DEATH DEFYING SK—It turned away.

Hilary stepped out, leaving her groceries in the booth. This booth was a temp, portable, one in a skewed line of four hooked with cables to stacks of batteries. Now she could see a sizeable yacht with piles of equipment on deck, surrounding a tube that resembled a cannon pointed straight up.

A woman in a business suit and flat shoes looked her over (seeing a child in party clothes) and said, "Hello, Dear. Who're you with? Let's see your invitation."

Hilary opened her purse and offered the card her parents insisted she carry, with her name, photo and home address. It wasn't what the official was expecting. "My jump card doesn't work right," she said.

The woman opened her mouth—and the crowd roared behind her. The cannon fired straight up. Something big disappeared from sight in a second or two, lost in a glare of clouds.

The woman—the greeter?—turned back. "A broken jump card? You came to the right place. Let's see that."

Hilary offered the bent jump card. "What's going on?"

"Publicity stunt," the woman said dismissively. "We sent Hosni LaSalle, the stunt man, through a spit cage. And I'm Willie Day, how do you do?"

"Hilary Firestone."

She was still holding both the calling card and the jump card. "Hilary, what did you do to this card?"

"A skateboard ran over it. Not my fault. Now—I thought it must be taking me to Points of Interest, you know, like with a Global Positioning System? There're cameras pointed at me wherever I go."

"There's a setting that does that. It's for newstapers," Willie said. "You're not supposed to have it. Hmm. You can't keep it. Maybe Mr. Whyte will be interested. We'll wait here until he's got a moment."

Hilary didn't quite like that, but—"Okay. I'll phone my parents." She fished her phone out of her belt pouch.

Willie Day took it before Hilary could react. "No, you certainly won't do that. This isn't a matter for the public."

Several options flicked through Hilary's mind. She could snatch the phone back. She could scream for help, with video cameras all around her. She could kick the woman in the kneecaps. She settled for snatching both cards out of her other hand, turning to enter the booth, and flicking out.

Hosni was still rising, rising … the cameras on his aeroshell were working fine. Clouds came at him and were torn apart. The sea dwindled below, the boat flotilla already lost. Voice was a little garbled. "If I had thought it through," Hosni said, "I would have gone through feet first. The thrust of the wind was all at my head end. I should have gone in upside down, with the fins at my ears."

Robin asked, "Are you all right?"

"Aye-firmative. So far so good. I think I'm in free fall now. Sky darkening, but you can see that yourself. How's the other thing going, Robin?"

Robin was facing several cameras; he made the most of it. "The *D. D. Harriman* is ready to launch. The spit cage in the tank is feeding hydrogen fuel. If this works out, we'll circle the Moon in a one-stage spacecraft. I know you'd have loved to be the pilot—"

"Oh, this is exciting enough, Boss. Time to drop the shell—"

"Hosni, I'll get back to you." Because Segundo Gomes of Security was listening hard to a cellphone, then barking into it. Robin punched out and went over. He asked, "Segundo? What?"

"Willie Day reports a young girl with a broken jump card. Coyote and—"

Robin took the phone. "Willie?"

"I take it you're looking for her. Coyote and Roadrunner T-shirt, active. She was on one of the observer boats, the *Hobbit*. Your engineering team might tell you how she got here. I took her phone, but she snatched the card back and flicked out."

"Did you damage *her* in any way?"

"No, Boss, I never touched her."

"And you have her phone. Good. Anything else?"

"Name's Hilary. And she said she's finding cameras everywhere she goes. I wondered—"

"Yeah. She's linked into a news feed, I bet. She goes wherever it's interesting. And she's got a link to … Willie, you'll know about this pretty quick, but it's secret. I've got an experimental setup going, called Long Jump mode, and her card seems to be using it."

Not long after dawn … or near sunset; how could you tell without directions?

Residential … but the signs were funny. Arabic? That nearest building was a church or synagogue or something religious and foreign. Hilary opened the booth door anyway, because that was a uniform, and the foreign-looking woman wasn't yet raising the gun in her right hand. Hilary called, "English?"

"Yes, of course," the woman said. "Please don't move. I want to see your hands."

"Where am I?"

"Jerusalem. Put the bag down with care."

Hilary knelt and began to set the bag down. Men were approaching, and they were all uniformed. "What's going on?"

"We have cleared these streets and closed reception on these booths. It should not have worked. How did you get past?"

"My card's damaged." She was surrounded now. "What's it all about?"

"The Gaza Seven Accords are to be signed. Peace in our time," the uniformed woman said with perhaps a touch of irony. "A fine opportunity for a homicide bomber."

Hilary suddenly saw herself as this officer must: an unexplained stranger with packages that could be bombs. She pulled the door shut and used the card. The Israeli was just a bit slow.

As before, she'd flicked out before she could type an address. She was looking at the Taj Mahal, right down the row of reflecting pools, the picture everybody sees first.

A moment later she saw the people. She was the only passenger in a row of booths, looking at a line of four bored, uniformed guards only just starting to react. Behind the guards was—everybody. The whole world. India. Some kind of celebration, dark skin and wonderful bright clothing, lots of children, cameras and shouting and signs.

Two dark-skinned guards stepped forward. "—," one said, and held out his hand. She saw the boredom fall away as he took in her armload of bags, the Western clothing.

She asked, "Speak English?"

He said, "Passport? Show me passport."

She screamed over the roar of voices. "I don't have it. I had no idea I was coming here."

"How you get here?" He was retreating. Other guards were pointing rifles at her.

Behind them there was a white flash, a sudden expanding cloud.

The blast flung them all forward. Hilary slammed the door against the blast. It slapped against the cage and Hilary.

She was sitting on the floor with her head ringing. A man was pulling the door open. He had a gun—a smallish machine gun, which he held one-handed—and he was grinning. The guards outside the booth were down, maybe shot. The gun stank of chemical fire.

He took her by the hair, pushed the gun into her throat, and asked, "American?"

"Yes." She stood up, carefully, following the pull of his hand.

"My card does not work. The police turn off the booths when a big event is run. Why does your card work? Does it?"

"It's broken. It takes me anywhere. Anywhere! I never have a choice." She was starting to cry. She handed him the card.

"Anywhere is good." He looked outside the booth. People were starting to move. He took it and inserted it into PAY.

The air gusted away. Hilary felt it leaving her lungs. She gasped. Darkness tried to shut down her mind, but the dark man's pull on her hair brought her back.

"What kind of jump card is this?" he asked, very faintly. Then, louder, "We should be frozen into ice. We've gone kilometers uphill. This is Everest!"

Hilary said, "That's impossible. There's no jump booth on Everest."

"Look." His grip eased a bit. "Someone left a sign. This is a temporary booth. It must have been lowered from a helicopter. God is great." The grip tightened. "Girl, what is this card?"

"I don't know. I don't know. It's not my fault."

The man looked at his own card, then put it away. "This will not take me anywhere. No booths close enough. Well, we'll try yours again." He pushed it into the PAY slot.

A roar like the end of the world flooded the booth.

The assassin flinched violently. Hilary didn't; she was ready for anything, including the flinch. She lunged up against the gun, flattened it against the booth wall with both hands, and pulled the man's trigger finger.

Whatever Whyte made these booths out of, it was way stronger than glass. Bullets bounced around the curve and into the assassin, up under his right shoulder. Hilary was screaming, the assassin was screaming, and neither could hear. Then the man had her by the throat with his left hand—but she had the gun. She turned it and fired again. He jerked, then sagged.

Outside, a great light was rising, rising. Nobody was looking at anything else. The noise was dropping toward a tolerable level.

And Hilary finally had a chance to think.

Where was she? Canaveral, of course. That rising flame must be *D. D. Harriman*, JumpShift's attempt at a spacecraft with its fuel source pumped from the ground. It seemed to be working. And the assassin seemed dead.

She let the man sag. He was wearing a western-style business suit. She patted the pockets. No wallet, no glasses, pockets all flat, wait, yes. A jump card.

Next: push her own bent card into the slot. Ready for anything.

The silence was deafening. The dark was absolute, barring the light in her booth. She opened the door a crack and caught a whiff of jungle vegetation.

Dark: she must be on the far side of the Earth. No way could a normal card get her home from here.

For an instant she considered tumbling the corpse outside—but no. Interfering with a crime scene had to be illegal. Instead she inserted her own damaged card again.

Rocks and a rustic one-story building; and the light looked right. Noon in California Sierras, maybe. Cross fingers and—

She pocketed her own bent card and inserted the assassin's. Her screen lit up. She punched the number she knew best.

Then she was gone.

Flick, flick, flick. Bump bump bump. The floor was punching up under her feet, so she must be going west ... not quite west, because she was hard up against one of the walls. She was sweating: that last place must have been in the mountains. The view flickered too much to tell anything else, except that the sun was nearly overhead.

Everything stopped.

Home. The sun was high, noonish.

The front door burst open and Mom stormed out. Mom was furious. She pulled open the booth door and waited for an explanation.

Hilary was propping a dead body against the wall. "I need the police," she said.

"Hilary, for God's sake! Is that blood?"

"It isn't mine. Mom, it's not exactly an emergency, and if I dial 911 they might hold me for hours. Should I flick to Morrow?" Wayne Morrow was their lawyer.

Mom said, "Yes, go to Wayne, for God's sake. Here, I'll come with you." Mom squeezed into the booth, biting her lip, her feet entangled with the dead man's. "What's that?"

"His jump card." It had a funny logo on it. "Mine doesn't work. Mom? We can't drag a bloody corpse into Wayne Morrow's office. He'd freak. Help me."

Mom got a cautious hold on the corpse, one that wouldn't leave much blood. They dragged the body out. Neither noticed when the booth door closed itself.

Then it was full of Willie Day and a uniformed man.

Day saw the corpse first. "Holy shit." Then Mom and Hilary. "Hilary, dear, we tracked you using your phone. Here," handing her the phone and turning to Mom. "And you are?"

JumpShift's man was kneeling over the corpse, feeling for a pulse, which was silly.

Mom said, "This is my home and you are an intruder. Who are *you*?"

"I work for JumpShift as a Security officer. I'm Willie Day. Your daughter has a card with unauthorized access, lots and *lots* of unauthorized access. We'd love to have her cooperation, and I expect she has a valid claim—"

"Lawsuit?"

"By the grace of God and a long-handled spoon, it may not come to that. Hilary, the corpse?"

"Set off a bomb at the Taj Mahal. Pushed that gun into my neck. Used my broken jump card. He kept his cool when we landed at Everest—yeah, Mom, *Everest!* But he freaked when he heard the rocket roaring in his head. That must have been the *D. D. Harriman*, right? I didn't freak. I shot him dead."

Mom started to stutter. "You. That card. Yours. We have a lawyer. I'm going to call him."

Officer Day frowned, but didn't interfere. "Good idea. And the police … may not have jurisdiction, but they'll claim it. Hilary, you've been very lucky and very clever too. Mrs. Firestone, I think we can satisfy you and Hilary and your lawyer too."

By the time the police were through with Hilary, she was exhausted. Mrs. Firestone took her home to sleep. She must have dealt with Mr. Firestone alone, and badly, because he was in the hospital with a mild heart condition.

The next day, Wanda and Hilary Firestone came to Jump-Shift's offices in Beverly Hills, with their lawyer.

Wayne Morrow was a tall, prematurely bald, lantern-jawed New Englander type from California. He examined Robin Whyte with the happy look of a new owner checking out an award-winning dog. Then he turned to JumpShift's lawyers, Nakamura and Dwayne.

"Before we can get down to cases," he said, "it would be well if you could tell us what exactly *happened* to Miss Firestone."

Dwayne said, "Much of this consists of internal secrets."

Robin said, "Truth is, we'll be telling some of those secrets to the media pretty soon. Not as soon as we would have without your, um, interference, Miss Firestone, but what the hell. Willie, you've tracked her path, haven't you?"

Security Officer Willie Day said, "We think so. Hilary, your card has been linked into the CNN news feed. From the Farmer's Market in Los Angeles you went first to the San Juan Islands. You could have quit there. Then to the Mojave, where you nearly got killed—"

"Hilary!" Mrs. Firestone shouted. Dwayne repressed a wince. Morrow's eyebrows went up, then he lost all expression.

"Testing an experimental teleport system has its dangers," Robin said. "We'll get to that."

"Then to Forest Lawn," Willie Day said. "Then the North Pole. Not dressed for that, were we? Then the market square in Ethiopia, then offshore from Spain, where we did the spit cage jump with Hosni. Then Jerusalem."

"I was lucky that cop spoke English."

"No, the Israelis teach English in their schools. Then India again, where they were doing a virtual tour for CNN, and that's where you picked up a hitchhiker, right?" Hilary nodded. Willie said, "Mount Everest. Girl, you're damned lucky the Boss's new system has a heat pump, not just the momentum transmitters."

"A little too much of that," Robin said, then, "Oh, what the hell. You'll have papers to sign to keep this confidential. Kid, we're developing a teleportation system that sends any momentum difference to a third target. It takes the bumps out of travel. I've been testing it myself, but nowhere near as drastically as you have. As Willie says, I put in a two-way heat pump so I won't freeze or broil when I go up and down."

Willie said, "Then you went to the Cape. That's where you shot the perp. He's the real thing, by the way. He set off a bomb in the CNN tour of the Taj Mahal. Twenty-four injured, six dead. When we tell this tale, you'll be a hero," Willie said, then looked at Robin. Was she assuming too much? "Then a retreat in Madagascar, then a lodge in the Sierras. That was when you used the perp's card and bounced home."

Morrow said, "You're telling us that you've endangered my client repeatedly."

Nakamura started to speak, but Robin cut him off. "Not quite. Hilary could have quit at the whale watch. Just called her parents. She knew she was using damaged equipment. Our disclaimers are specific here. She'd have missed all the fun, of course. Hilary, why didn't you do that?"

Hilary didn't answer.

Mrs. Firestone said, warningly, "Hilary?"

Hilary said clearly, "Dad and Mom never let me go anywhere."

There was laughter. Robin Whyte said, "Of course you're entitled to compensation."

"Quite a lot, I think. You endangered my client—"

"I saved her too, but never mind," Robin said. "She's done us some good. We're examining the jump card; we'll get something out of that. We can get huge amounts of data about the new system by tracking her path. Dialing at random—yes, dear, I know you didn't actually dial, but the card was doing that for you. You went places I'd never have dared. Flicked halfway around the world. You do that at the equator and you land running at half a mile per second."

For the first time since he'd met her, the girl looked scared.

About time, he thought. "What I'm getting at is," Robin said, "I'd like you to take the same package Hosni LaSalle gets. As a test pilot."

Hilary looked … yeah, *she'd* bought it. The lawyer Morrow was saying, "How much is that in money?"

"He gets a flat two hundred thousand for the stunt, plus some perks. You'd be paid for any publicity resulting from this deal, and, Hilary, there's likely to be a lot. We'll want you as a spokesperson. Let you in on more of what we're doing. Newstaper interviews. Probably *The Tonight Show.*"

Morrow said, "If a jury got hold of this—"

Dwayne said, "*Or* we could countersue. She knowingly used damaged—"

"I'm in," Hilary said. "Mom?"

"Oh, dear. Your father will freak."

About Brad R. Torgersen

I first met Brad Torgersen in 2010 when I handed him a trophy for being a Finalist at the Writers of the Future Contest. We became friends, collaborated on three stories for various anthologies, and I was thrilled to see him make the Campbell ballot for Best New Writer, and receive both Hugo and Nebula nominations in 2012, incredibly early in his career for such honors.

Along the way I learned that his favorite writer, the one whose work inspired him to become a science fiction writer, was Larry Niven. And since Larry had also judged Writers of the Future and was acquainted with Brad's work, I suggested to Larry that we break our six-book precedent and give him two protégés. He graciously agreed.

And while Brad was writing his share of this book, he also sold his first collection and his first novel. This is a young man with a truly promising future in the science fiction field.

Mike Resnick

BOOK THREE:
SPARKY THE DOG

BRAD R. TORGERSEN

"BARRY?" ASKED THE WITHERED OLD MAN in the bed.

"I'm surprised you called after the dinner hour," replied a much younger man—who'd poked his head through the old man's bedroom door.

"Come on in," the old man said, beckoning.

Barry Jerome Jansen walked quietly to the side of the adjustable-geometry mattress where his friend lay. Robin Whyte was thin. Far thinner than the previous time Jerryberry had seen him. Not a hair on the old man's head, nor any eyebrows either. Liver spots covered the billionaire to the point that he appeared leopard-like.

As penthouse apartments went, Rob's was palatial. Statues from China and Rome. Marble from Greece. A plush, hand-woven carpet from Southeast Asia. But even the old man's grand style couldn't quite mask the lingering scents of long-delayed decay: disinfectants, rubbing alcohol, half a dozen different ointments, and the undeniably telltale aroma of living flesh that's spent one too many years clinging to its owner's bones.

"What's the occasion?" Jerryberry asked, specifically working to keep his nose from wrinkling.

"You know me," Rob said. "When I get an idea, I hate to sit on it. Especially these days. Not much time left."

Longevity treatments—the exotic kind only available to the richest of the rich—had allowed Robin Whyte to push well past one hundred and twenty years. But then cancer had ultimately caught up with him, and he was now too frail for the chemo and radiation therapy that might have slowed the metastases.

"You're looking good," Jerryberry said, mustering a smile.

"Cut the crap," Rob replied, laughing quietly, which began a small fit of coughing. Jerryberry eyed the large, red panic button at the bed's side, then saw the remote medical cameras that oversaw the whole room, and decided that the in-home nurses would come when the in-home nurses would come. They didn't need Jerryberry playing doctor for them.

Besides, Rob never called unless it was for business reasons.

"How's the exposé coming?" Rob asked.

"Post-production is going great. We've got over three hours of footage, photos, interviews, all of it gelling nicely. With the big anniversary of JumpShift coming up, it's been a good time to be a newstaper—at least one with exclusive access."

"Good," Rob said. "I look forward to seeing my program when it airs. Did you bring the camera like I asked?"

Jerryberry held up the small case he carried: portable tripod, with palm-sized digital recording device, and attendant microphone.

"Deathbed confessions?" Jerryberry said, half-joking.

"You might call them that," Rob replied. "Go ahead and get your stuff set up. The doc tells me I've got weeks. Maybe, days. I've liked living longer than most, but even I have to admit: getting this old *sucks*."

"I'm not exactly a spring chicken myself," Jerryberry chided him. "Or have you gone so blind you didn't notice the silver in my hair?"

"Better to have silver on the dome, than nothing at all," Rob said. "My ex-wife told me that."

"Which one?"

"Karolyn," Rob said. "The only woman—of the three— who actually loved me. God rest her soul."

"How long has it been now?" Jerryberry asked, setting the tripod up at the foot of the bed and adjusting the camera's ambient lighting sensitivity for best picture quality.

"Too long," Rob said.

"Okay, we're good to go," Jerryberry said. The little blue light on top of the device told them both that the digital camera was recording steadily. Jerryberry would obviously cut and edit later, for salient content. Whatever Rob ultimately approved for public release, per their tacit arrangement.

"Have a seat," Rob said, pointing to the nearby chair. Jerryberry sat down and pulled the chair close to the bed, so that he could look Rob in the eye without blocking the camera's angle.

"When we did the bulk of the interviews," Rob said, licking his lips, "I made sure to include all of the exciting stuff from the early days. The research. The scoffers in the academy. Breakthroughs. Even some of the mishaps."

"Like the girl?" Jerryberry said, grinning.

Rob chuckled. "Poor Hilary! Yes, like her. But what I didn't tell you was the one thing I didn't *dare* tell until I was sure that I wouldn't care who found out—because I'll be gone soon."

"Okay, that sounds juicy enough," Jerryberry said.

Rob's eyes suddenly glazed over and he rested his head on his pillow, staring up at the ceiling—which was mostly glass. The orange light of sunset glowed beautifully on the bellies of several small clouds.

"We were working in the Mojave," the old man said. "Lightspeed Labs. I've taken you there before. Only this was in the very beginning, before we ever sold a single commercial booth. Before JumpShift became what it is now. Daniella— my first wife—hated the desert. Wouldn't come out of her social cocoon in San Francisco unless I begged her. Resented the fact that I was spending whole weeks on the company clock, at the Labs, trying to nurse my idea—cost-effective, instant teleportation—toward reality ..."

***

Dr. Rob Whyte was in his late thirties. Fit. Ambitious. And ready to show his dream to the world.

After the success of the year-long test program which had sent pots and pans and all manner of other household objects *flicking* from one teleportation booth at one end of the lab, to its twin on the other end, and back, the time had come for the rubber to meet the road.

A handful of adventurous grad students—on loan from Cal Tech—had been *flicking* each other from place to place around the Mojave. Each time, they'd moved the booths and extended the range; while also noticing the turbulence that resulted from conservation of energy and momentum: the further apart the booths were, the greater the jump, bump, or stumble that resulted at the end.

Rob had a notion about that. Extending the booths to the range necessary to make them commercially appealing was a significant practical problem. Enough so that he began sketching digital designs on his e-pad: great, bobbing spheroids of metal, each suspended in a liquid buffer like Lake Tahoe in the Sierras, or the Great Salt Lake in Utah, or the Pacific Ocean off the coast of California if it came to it. Hook them up to the teleportation grid, use them to bleed off the energy mid-flick …

But, first things first. Rob had a very important skeptic to convince. Someone who'd been dubious about his passion from the start, despite the fact that his startup company had attracted enough speculative investors to keep Mrs. Whyte comfortably housed and fed in one of the most expensive cities in the United States.

Daniella Veracruz Whyte was stern-faced as Rob ushered her into the main lab area that housed the "home booth" of the fledgling JumpShift teleportation network. Shaped like a huge test tube with its bottom up, the booth was unremarkable save for the button-clustered control module that sat at about ribcage level in the booth's interior.

Half a dozen twins of the booth were scattered around the government-leased, thousand-acre campus of Lightspeed

Labs. The plan was to take Daniella on a "tour" of the system, small as it might be. To show her that Rob's madness was, in fact, genius after all. That they weren't going to become paupers when the investors ran out and the company folded up into a colossal stone around their necks.

"You'll see," Rob said, waving his hand with a flourish while half a dozen other technicians and assistants—most of them associates and friends from Rob's days as a grad student himself—respectfully got to their feet.

Daniella seemed unimpressed.

"Robin," she said, "it's been a long day, and I am tired. Can we please just get this over with?"

"Of course my dear, of course. But I think you'll be quite surprised. This is the main booth—the one I've been telling you about since it was just an idea in my head, back before we met. Over against that far wall is Booth Two; the second prototype. There are a few more just like them placed here and there. I estimate that with quick dialing we ought to be able to complete the circuit in five minutes. If you would, please ..."

Daniella stared suspiciously at Rob's hand, which motioned for her to step toward Booth One.

"No," she said.

"I beg your pardon, my dear?"

"No, Robin."

"It's perfectly safe," he said. "We've had people flicking in and out of the booths for many days now. Hundreds of trips. Short, and not so short. It's instantaneous. And painless. I've done it myself more than once. Trust me. You won't be disappointed."

But Daniella wouldn't budge.

Rob looked down at Sparky, the short-legged Labrador-Basset mix who was Daniella's constant companion. His leash was wrapped firmly in her hand while he gratefully laid his belly on the AC-cooled tiles of the lab floor, his pink tongue just slightly sticking out as he panted. This time of the year, the Mojave was blisteringly hot. No place for a canine with any sanity, Rob thought.

"If I may," Rob said, trying to take the leash from Daniella's hands.

"Don't even think about—"

"Daniella," Rob said, "you've been worrying and complaining about this for many months. That this project—the company—was a dead-end. At least allow me to prove to you that JumpShift *works*. That it's going to make every man and woman in this room *rich*."

Daniella's grip on the leash remained iron-strong.

"Animal testing is cruel, Robin. You know how I feel about that sort of thing. Putting Sparky in that contraption would be like putting a small child into it. What if something *happens*?"

"Like I said," Rob persisted, working to keep his voice calm, "I've had people using the system already. It's absolutely safe. Now, I perfectly understand your hesitation to step into the booth yourself, because you haven't been here to see the results before. So at least let me demonstrate the system's harmlessness? The dog won't get so much as a scratch."

Daniella's fist remained clamped on the leash.

"Please?" Rob said, looking directly into his wife's eyes. "You know I'm as fond of this dog as you are. For God's sake, Daniella, I wouldn't put Sparky through anything I wasn't willing to experience myself."

Slowly, she relaxed her hand, and Rob gently guided the amiable dog over to the interior of Booth One, where he told Sparky to sit, then fed him a small dog treat, and unhooked the leash. Well-trained by one of the best handlers in the Bay Area, Sparky complied perfectly, crunching his treat with gusto and watching passively as Dr. Whyte walked several paces to the main computer workstation that monitored and controlled the booths.

"Should I cover my eyes?" Daniella said.

"Nothing so dramatic," Rob said, grinning. "First you see him there, and suddenly you see him—"

Rob tapped a few keys, then aimed a finger at Booth Two.

"—over *there*."

Sparky had vanished from Booth One.

But Booth Two remained empty. Not even a tell-tale gust of air puffing out, as was sometimes the case during teleportation.

Rob's smile fell.

Daniella's expression began to turn murderous.

"Where in the hell did you—"

Rob cut her off, reaching for his cell phone and dialing quickly.

"Station Three," he said, "I just tried to send my wife's dog through to Booth Two. Did you get him instead?"

A moment of silence, then one of the grad students reported, "No sir, not a sign of anyone, nor any dog for that matter."

Rob hung up and dialed Station Four.

Same result.

Station Five … Station Six …

"You've *vaporized* him!" Daniella accused. Her hands were clenched at her sides and her arms shook with outrage. She looked as if she was going to take a swing at her husband.

Lightspeed Labs personnel scattered, slamming their butts into chairs in front of computers—keys being tapped frantically while they tried to unearth the nature of the malfunction.

Rob closed his eyes and pinched his fingers over the bridge of his nose.

"Sparky is not vaporized," he said, ruing the fact that an obvious technical glitch—Murphy's Law—had selected this moment in history to manifest itself.

"Then *where* is my dog, Robin?" Daniella demanded.

"Somewhere," Rob said. "Just not here. The booths don't destroy matter. They merely shift it from place to place. There always has to be a sender and a receiver. The booths just can't magically materialize you anywhere, out of thin air."

"So where is this *extra* booth?" Daniella asked, her arms now crossed over her California-implanted breasts. "If I don't get Sparky back this instant I'm going to take it out of your ass, Robin! That dog is my baby! That dog is—"

"Perfectly safe," Rob finished for her.

"Where??" Daniella said, her face turning bright pink.

Rob continued to pinch his nose. Suddenly he looked up. "Let's find out."

Moving so quickly that nobody could stop him, Dr. Whyte strode directly over and into Booth One. He pressed the orange SEND button, without dialing anything otherwise. That way the booth was guaranteed to transport him immediately to wherever Sparky had gone. For a split second Rob had the good sense to experience fear. The image of his scowling, excellently-manicured wife was replaced by the dimly-lit confines of what appeared to be an unfinished residential basement.

An invisible force seemingly caused Dr. Whyte to lurch into the strange receiver's wall. He fell to his knees. *Long jump*, he thought. *Too long?* Rob painfully got back to his feet and took a good look out of the receiver's door—its walls were opaque, unlike the transparent booths Lightspeed Labs had been pioneering.

Three men were clustered around a desk festooned with computer equipment that trailed cables up to the booth proper.

One of them yelled at the top of his lungs for *that goddamned dog to shut up.*

Sparky skipped and danced around in front of the booth, his throaty, deep bark belying his otherwise diminutive size.

These were not people Rob knew.

One of them turned to him, and aimed a fist—with a pistol in it.

"That's what I'd call a 'check your shorts' moment," Jerryberry said, his eyebrows raised as he stared at Rob, who still lay on his pillows, his eyes gazing up and out into the darkening sky. There would be stars soon. With the advent of viable teleportation technology, much of California's smog-inducing transportation system had become obsolete. No more cars, trucks, or buses. The day the last of the haze cleared from the L.A. skies, it had been international news. Just like in Salt Lake City, and Mexico City, and Beijing after that, and so on and so forth. Everywhere the JumpShift booths were put into wide use, the skies had cleared.

"I nearly peed myself," Rob said, smiling weakly at the memory.

"So how the heck did you wind up in someone else's lab?" Jerryberry asked.

"To call it a 'lab' is being too generous," Rob said. "It was a safe house. And those men? They weren't grad students."

"Hands up," the man with the pistol said.

Rob reflexively raised his palms over his head, his eyes scanning the interior of the opaque booth with a mixture of curiosity and fear.

Sparky continued to bark loudly, snarling low and guttural, deep in his thick throat.

"Just shoot the bugger," one of the other men said.

"No, wait," Rob said, "I can get him to stop."

"Do it," said the man with the gun.

Rob whistled once, and called Sparky over to him. The dog glared at the strangers for an instant, then waddled over on his outsized paddle-like Basset feet and huddled against Rob's legs. The Doctor reached down and scratched the mongrel pet's ears, then patted Sparky on his side reassuringly.

"Do we know him?" asked the man with the pistol.

One of the others turned and walked up to the receiver.

"Yes," the second man said. "I've seen his photos on the JumpShift web site. It's the goddamned company founder."

The man with the pistol whistled loudly.

"So what's the scheme?" Rob asked, his hands still up. "Money? I can assure you that JumpShift doesn't have much to spare. All of our capital is tied up in equipment and assets at this time. If you're planning to get rich off JumpShift, I'd encourage you to send me back—no questions asked—then invest in stock once we go public in a few months."

The man with the gun smiled, and sniffed laughter: derision.

"I'm totally serious," Rob said.

"I know that," said the third man, who until now had been entirely focused on his computer screen. He turned, so that his face could finally be seen, and Rob blinked twice.

"Kevin?"

"How you doin', Rob?"

"Trying to avoid my wife's fiery wrath," Rob said. "How are you doing, *Doctor* Tanner?"

"Oh, so-so," the third man said.

All of them were wearing blue jeans and white T-shirts. With black tennis shoes. No watches. Nothing that could have distinguished them in a crowd, nor given Rob any clue whatsoever as to where he was.

"I didn't expect you to be the one who came walking into my web," Kevin said.

"Oh? What precisely *did* you expect?"

"I've been watching pots and pans blip in and out of my booth for a long time now. We turned it off for a while, to refine the programming on the big-neutrino network interrupt I've created, and only went live again this morning. I was expecting more hardware to blip through. But then your mutt showed up, followed quickly by yourself. I'm happy to report that our adjustments obviously paid off. Our prototype works beautifully."

"The booths must have precisely the same volume," Rob said. "Down to the final cubic millimeter. Otherwise they won't work. The test subject simply stays put. No teleport. I am figuring you didn't just make a lucky guess. Someone on the inside—on my end—has to have been passing you information."

The buzz from numerous computer fans filled the air, while Sparky's gentle panting could he heard at Rob's feet. The other men were stone-faced, but fidgety. Kevin and Rob were being far too civil. A tremor of violence still lurked in the air, waiting to be unleashed.

"Yes and no," Kevin said. "Back in school you were very eager to share your ideas with the rest of us. Most might have thought you were nuts, but I actually kept some of your more detailed drawings and computer files you e-mailed me. I hung onto them. When news of JumpShift's existence hit the technical community, I decided you might not be crazy after all. I went to work by myself. With a little effort and some try-and-fail, I eventually got the size and shape of the booth right. Figuring out the receiver took some intuition—along with some help from these fine gentlemen. But again, you were prone to sharing your ideas."

"So now you're an industrial crook," Rob said, his hands dropping. "What happened with the big IPO venture up in Seattle that was going to make you millions?"

"It was a gamble," Kevin said. "A bad one."

"And you went broke," Rob said. "So now you're trying to pirate my technology? What good will it do you? Especially now that someone you're working with has a gun pointed at me, and I can reasonably identify all of you for the cops?"

"You said it yourself, there *is* someone on the inside."

"I'd give a finger or two to know who."

"You won't like the answer," Kevin said with a dour smile.

"Try me," Rob replied.

"In a minute maybe. Let's go back to what you said earlier, about stock. JumpShift is going on the market? Do you think you're that ready?"

"We need the capital to get the booths into the wider world. As many as possible, as quickly as possible. Unless or until we can make the booths ubiquitous, they will be an industrial curiosity. Just like wireless phones and e-pads, we need people to *need* the booths."

"A booth in every garage?" Kevin said.

"Just about."

Rob felt himself sweating under his shirt. The air in the basement was cool, but with that gun aimed at him, Rob's heart rate remained at triple-time. Sparky stayed more or less calm, but if either of the two strangers made any sudden moves, Rob knew—from long experience—that it would set the dog off again. Which might prompt the man with the pistol to begin putting holes in things, as well as people.

"Your best option," Rob said, trying to keep his voice controlled, "is to send my dog and I back through the way we came."

"Just like that?" Kevin said. "No harm, no foul? Obviously you've got a major problem now that you know someone with the right knowledge can hack into your booth network."

"Obviously," Rob said.

"Have any idea yet how I did it?"

"Not especially, no."

"Then that knowledge is worth something."

Rob smiled slightly, and began to nod his head. *Ah.* Very clever. His old buddy from Cal Tech had lost a small mint up north, and come crawling back to California with his hat in his hand. Unable to buy stock outright, Kevin was trying to extort his way into the JumpShift circle—either Rob adopted Kevin as a technical partner, with full shares, or Rob might be left scratching his head over the problem of how someone outside JumpShift had managed to produce a booth capable of shoehorning in on the JumpShift network.

Unless the JumpShift booths could be proven to work safely *and* securely, the public would not trust them to the extent Rob needed the public to trust them, in order for Jump-Shift booths to reach the tipping point of saturation necessary for them to change the economy.

"Ballsy," Rob said to his old friend. Especially since Rob and Kevin had had a rather nasty falling out when Daniella first came on the scene.

"How much do your henchmen get?"

Kevin smiled without humor.

"A full cut. Dave and Mike were at school with us. A year or two back. You wouldn't remember them because you barely paid attention to what was in front of your nose at that time. They lost money in Seattle too. I convinced them that we could combine our efforts and obtain a reasonable slice of the

JumpShift pie, and all we'd have to do is put in some after-office hours. As well as a little cash for the hardware."

"And if I refuse?" Rob said.

"Don't refuse," said the man with the gun.

"I'm not worth anything to you dead," Rob said.

"Don't be so sure," Kevin said.

"You seriously went there?" Jerryberry asked.

"Yup," Rob replied. "Standing there in that booth I realized that I had something they all desperately wanted, and as long as I could take it away from them, I had the real source of control. Gun in my face or no gun in my face."

"But Kevin was right," Jerryberry said. "You did leave a major technical string hanging, on account of him having been able to pick his way into your system with apparently so little difficulty. Obviously the booth systems are secure. Now. Otherwise nobody would use them. Did you eventually invest in more R&D and get it figured out?

"Hang on," Rob said, holding a hand up. "The plot's about to thicken."

Dr. Whyte slowly trudged up the narrow stairway that led from the basement to the upper floor. The man with the pistol—Mike—was at Rob's back. Sparky clambered along at Rob's heel, obediently going wherever Rob did. At the top of the stairs Rob opened the door and found himself in the run-down kitchen of a turn-of-the-century rambler. A grimy sink was filled with dirty dishes, and the adjacent dining and family rooms were empty, save for a few folding chairs and a folding card table that was similarly heaped with dirty dishes.

"One of you needs to page room service," Rob joked.

"We don't come here to vacation," Mike said.

Rob chanced a look out the back window, over the sink.

There was desert for as far as he could see: beige sand, scrub brush, and in the distance, a couple of lonely Joshua trees.

Not too far off, Rob noted to himself. That they were still somewhere in or at the edges of the Mojave told him what he needed to know about how much distance he'd actually crossed. Surely it had been the biggest shift yet taken. It also suggested that Kevin's loophole technology might be proximity-based. Nobody could simply jack into the network from out-system unless they were very close to the system's origin. Good. That might make it simpler to fix the security bug, assuming Rob ultimately found a way to get back to Lightspeed Labs.

Kevin and the other one, Dave, came up behind Mike.

"Nobody at JumpShift will trust any of you any further than you could be thrown," Rob said. "Even if all you're after is twenty thousand shares of free stock."

"Trust is not the question," Kevin said. "It's not personal. It's business. You might discover how I cracked your network, or you might not. Dare you go live with your technology on the open market when I can sell *my* booth to a competitor? Especially if *my* booths can tap into *your* proprietary network? The way I see it, either you work with me, and live, or you don't work with me, and … well, a lot of bad things can happen in the desert."

"Daniella isn't liable to turn over the life insurance money," Rob said, chuckling—despite the circumstances.

Dave's eyes swiveled to Kevin's, who glanced at Rob, then glanced to the ceiling.

A little creeping sensation went up Rob's spine.

"Wait a minute—"

"She's a beautiful woman," Kevin said. "It's a shame you let her languish in San Francisco while you're out here practically all year long, slaving away. A lady can get … lonely. Under those circumstances.

Shit.

It suddenly made sense.

And among their small circle of social friends, Daniella was the only one who'd known what her trip to Lightspeed Labs was all about. And on this particular day, too. Kevin had said he'd only turned his booth back on this morning. There was never a guarantee that Rob would be the one stepping through the booth and into Kevin's erstwhile basement hideout. But on the chance that it *would* be Rob …

Rob suddenly felt sick to his stomach. He'd trusted Daniella, as any good husband should. And she'd betrayed that trust. In more ways than one.

But he wasn't going to let his feelings show in front of his captors.

Resisting the urge to vomit, Rob gritted his teeth and spoke.

"The perfect alibi. Bravo. Estranged wife watches as husband chases pooch into scary gizmo. Poof. Dog and husband vanish. Nobody knows where. Industrial accident. The body stays in the desert, far away from where anyone might look. Widow and widow's boyfriend collect the substantial check from the insurance company."

"And the boyfriend marries the widow, goes on to help the widow stabilize the company, perfect the technology, Jump-Shift still goes on the market, yadda, yadda, yadda. See, Rob, this whole thing has a happy ending for me no matter what. There is but one and only one way for there to be a happy ending for *you*."

"So it would seem."

Just then Sparky began to whine through his nose. Little whistling squeaks.

"What now?" Mike said, irritated.

"When a dog's gotta pee," Rob said.

The three kidnappers looked at each other.

"The damn mutt can't piddle in here," Kevin said. "This place stinks enough as it is. Take it outside."

When Dave reached down to grab Sparky's collar, the dog snarled and snapped at Dave, who yanked his hand away and backed off a couple of steps. He looked at Kevin, who seemed to be deciding if he was going to let Mike shoot the dog of his lover.

"Just take us both outside," Rob said. "I need some fresh air, and time to think about this. Obviously you're prepared to wait for an answer?"

"Obviously," Kevin said. "Mike? Will you do the honors?"

Mike prodded Rob through the kitchen to the door that led out into the garage, which was almost dark. Flicking on the garage light, Mike then prodded Rob through the back door and out into the back yard. Which was really just a fenced-in area filled with tumbleweeds and sand.

Rob led Sparky over by the fence proper, where Sparky began to sniff around the posts, occasionally lifting his leg and sending yellow streams into the dry dirt.

Mike kept the pistol on Rob the whole time.

Though he himself had not spent much time using guns of any sort, Rob got the sense that Mike wasn't exactly comfortable with the weapon.

Sparky finished up and began panting heavily, the desert still being hot despite the fact that the sun was starting to drift down to the western horizon.

"Got a water bowl handy?" Rob asked.

"No," Mike said.

"The dog needs *agua*."

"I don't care," Mike said sternly.

Rob spied a spigot on the rear exterior of the house—which, now that Rob could get a better look, appeared to be the only home on a lonely one-lane road for many miles in any direction.

"At least let me try my luck with that," Rob said, pointing to the spigot. "You might not think the well water in these parts is good enough to do dishes with, but it will at least wet Sparky's whistle."

Mike glared at Rob, then nodded.

Rob walked quickly back to the garage and spied inside for a bowl or container of any description. He saw a stack of rusty hubcaps piled in a corner, retrieved one of them, then walked back outside—Mike's pistol trained on Rob's torso the whole time—and worked the round handle on the spigot.

Gloppy, silt-mired water sputtered forth.

Rob let it run for a few seconds until reasonably clean water began to spill onto the ground, at which point he filled up the hubcap, then bent over to set it on the ground in front of Sparky, who promptly and eagerly began to lap.

Rob wiped an arm across his brow, feeling the dampness forming at his neck and in the pits of his arms.

"I picked a hell of a place to work my wonders," Rob said to no one in particular.

"You should have picked Sacramento," Mike said grudgingly. "Between the heat, and the time, and the expense, this whole deal has been a colossal pain in my ass."

"Didn't want to spook anyone in the city," Rob said honestly. "People get nervous when you play with prototype tech near population centers."

When Sparky had lapped the hubcap empty, Rob went back to the spigot for more.

He filled the hubcap.

"Aw dammit," Rob suddenly said.

"What?" Mike asked.

"C'mere, look,"

Mike took two steps.

Rob flung the hubcap full of water as hard as he could.

Mike stumbled back and away, both hands raised to protect his face. The cloudy water sloshed across him, but by then Rob had pounced. He'd done a bit of wrestling in high school, and while his moves were rusty, his physique was not.

The gun was out of Mike's hand and Rob had Mike in a choke-hold within five seconds, the two men struggling against each other while Sparky began to bark and snarl, snapping teeth at Mike's feet as Mike kicked them out desperately, fingers clawing at the muscular arm locked around his throat.

"Hey!" a voice shouted from the garage door.

Dave.

Not wanting to find out if either Kevin or Dave had brought an additional gun, Rob threw Mike to the ground, scooped up Mike's pistol, and bolted for the back gate, which he kicked open so hard the wood splintered and the gate hung by one hinge.

Sparky bolted out ahead of Rob as Rob ran into the setting sun.

Jerryberry wasn't quite sure what to say. He'd been a newstaper for practically his entire adult life. He'd covered his share of crime and hijinks in that period. But never had he heard of anything quite so unique as what he was hearing now. It wasn't just industrial espionage. It wasn't just extortion. It wasn't just a jilted spouse playing off the lover against the husband. It was a pot-boiled pastiche of all three things. To the point that Jerryberry sat back in his chair, his mouth screwed up in a skeptical pucker.

"You think I've got my fingers crossed behind my back," Rob said.

"I didn't say that."

"You didn't have to."

"Well, taken from my perspective—the steely-eyed, pointy end of journalism—a story like this is a little hard to swallow. Before I let any of this get into the exposé, I'd have to do some fact-checking first."

"You think I'm out-and-out lying?"

"Not at all," Jerryberry said, placing a calming hand on Rob's shoulder, which despite being painfully bony, had gone tight with tension. "I just want to make sure that I can answer all the same questions that an astute viewer would begin to ask: where are Kevin, Mike, and Dave now? What about Daniella? What did you do with her after you—"

"Shut up, and I'll tell you the rest of it. One thing I never did like about newstapers: you guys always want to ask too many questions at the wrong time."

"Remember the mall riot?" Jerryberry said.

"What about it?"

"My asking too many questions at the wrong time on that one got the laws and the technology changed. We don't have riots like that anymore. Nor the looting that went with them. JumpShift was able to spare itself a legal *and* PR backlash as a result."

"Don't pat yourself on the back too hard," Rob said. "You were in the dark until I decided to take pity on you, and help you out."

"We helped *each other* out, final analysis."

"Okay, I guess maybe we did."

"Which is why we've been friends ever since."

"Yeah, well, there is that. Listen, Barry, I'm being totally honest."

"Okay, so you're being totally honest. How in the hell did you manage to make it out of the desert alive? Even if Kevin or his guys didn't have another gun, where was there for you to go? Sounds like you were on the Nevada side, by my reckoning. Nothing but heat and parched earth for miles and miles."

"You're right about that," Rob said. "After I took off running, I got a better look at the countryside, and it was bleak. And unlike Sparky, I hadn't gotten a bellyful of fluid. My tongue turned to cotton in my mouth. I had to find a dry creek bed and duck down in it to catch my breath. Maybe a mile from the house. And I could see they were out combing for me. I knew it wouldn't be long until they caught up."

"Was there a car in the driveway? Something you circle back for, and use to make an escape?"

"No," Rob said. "Which, in a way, gave me an idea."

Dr. Whyte followed the dry creek bed, sometimes crouched almost onto all fours, until he hit the raised road. A two-meter-diameter corrugated pipe ran under the road, allowing rain water to pass through without washing away the road base during thunderstorms. He beckoned Sparky in, sat down—grateful for the shade—and tried to think. With no wheels and no way to flick back to Lightspeed Labs, he had precious few options.

But then he'd seen no car in the garage, and unless his far-distance vision was playing tricks on him, no car in the driveway either. Nor any cars passing on the road during the time it had taken Rob to get to the culvert.

Sparky panted at Rob's feet.

On impulse, he reached down and mussed the dog's head, causing Sparky's long ears to toss about clownishly.

"Any thoughts, my friend?" Rob said.

Sparky *woofed* in the negative.

"Okay, but maybe I do. And it seriously bums me out, to be honest. We're going to have to go back to that house, one way or another. Kevin's got a second booth he's not telling me about. It's the only way he's been able to get out here, though I have to wonder about his power source."

A line of elderly power poles ran up and down the side of the road: a lonely black-wrapped electrical wire spiraled around a steel cable, which hung from the poles' crossbars.

Heck of a utility bill, Rob thought.

Or had Kevin rigged up a heck of a battery room?

Rob pulled out the pistol and made sure the safety was on before he disengaged the little magazine and pulled the slide back, dropping the chambered round into his hand. 9 millimeter. Beretta. A policeman's weapon. Army too, from what Rob remembered.

He looked at the gun and sighed.

Could Dr. Robin Whyte, physicist and would-be techno-tycoon, take another human life?

He guessed he now had about a 50/50 chance of finding out.

Using the opposite side of the road as cover, Rob slow-crouched his way back toward the house. Sparky trailed obediently and, thankfully, with very little noise. Every now and again Rob stopped to put his ear to the wind, listening for the crunch of shoes or boots up on the gravel shoulder.

Nothing.

Once he was satisfied that the house was within as easy reach as could be gotten, Rob laid down on the other side of the road—the raised slope concealing him, he hoped—and waited for dusk.

He'd stand a much better chance getting across the road unseen if he did it in the dark.

They waited. And waited. Sparky curled up at Rob's side and closed his eyes, seemingly thankful for the shade. The sun sank lower, and lower, and finally slipped behind the horizon.

Before long, Rob shivered. He'd forgotten that it got cold in the desert at night.

Believing that it was now or never, Rob got back into a crouch and fast-walked across the road, up the empty driveway, and to the side of the brick-built garage. Sidling along with his back to the still-warm wall, Rob noticed a cement stairwell leading down to the basement floor below. He crept down the steps, his ears like radar dishes, waiting for the mildest peep that would indicate he was blown.

Nothing.

The handle on the door at the bottom wouldn't budge.

Locked. Naturally.

Rob cursed his luck, when he noticed the grubby old mat at the bottom of the stairwell.

Not that easy, Rob thought.

He peeled the mat back and, by feel, discovered the key on the drain grate underneath.

It fit into the door lock with a bit of effort—no graphite had been applied to the knob's workings in a long time—then Rob twisted the knob very gently, very gently …

CLICK!

Rob froze. The door had popped open in an obnoxiously loud fashion.

Inside, it was pitch black.

Still no noise.

Had Kevin and his helpers actually remained in the desert looking for their escaped prisoner? Rob silently prayed that they'd gotten lost when the sun went down. He'd need the time to figure out Kevin's computer system, and either find a way to flick back to Kevin's other receiver, or to the Lightspeed Labs. Assuming Rob's fellows back at Lightspeed hadn't torn the booth network apart—trying to discover the error that had erased their boss.

But the Lightspeed crew knew the facts as well as Rob did. The booth technology was safe precisely because nobody got caught "in transport" only to have his or her molecules dispersed randomly. The giant neutrino either bounced to a target booth, or it reflected back. One, or the other. Somewhere, somehow, a man materialized. Every time. It was essential to the physics of the whole operation. Physics Rob had first come to understand while dawdling as a fourth-year student, just prior to picking a grad-school major.

Hopefully someone at Lightspeed had left Booth One functional, at the very least.

Rob crept through the dark space. He desperately wanted to find a light switch, but the bare cement walls were not encouraging. Occasionally he nosed into bare wood studding, stubbing a toe or bruising his knuckles.

Suddenly he saw the light.

Under a door.

Rob eased up to it.

Just as he reached his hand for the knob, a terrific commotion of *BARK-BARK-BARK-BARK* came from upstairs. Outside.

Rob realized that Sparky had not followed him into the house.

To hell with it!

Rob grabbed the knob to the inner door and, when it wouldn't yield, threw all his weight against it with his shoulder.

The wooden door's jamb burst, and the door flew open.

Kevin's booth sat empty.

The computer ran, its monitor dancing with geometric shapes.

Dear Lord, please don't let the screensaver be password-protected!

Rob waggled the mouse and was relieved to see the screen return to its normal self. A custom GUI interface showed numbers and graphs not too dissimilar from the kind Rob had been used to seeing back at Lightspeed Labs.

Footfalls. Heavy ones. Rushing into the back of the house. *BARK-BARK-BARK-BARK-BARK!*

There was no time. The feet were coming down the inner stairs.

Rob clicked a large green GUI button that simply said HOME and ran for the booth. He stepped into it and stared around dumbly, looking for the dialer just as he would have done inside a JumpShift booth. It had to be there, right? Right??

The feet were off the stairs.

Rob pulled out the pistol and worked the slide, taking the safety off.

Kevin, Mike, and Dave flew into the room. Two of them had shotguns, though not at the ready.

Rob aimed squarely at them.

"You have clumsy henchmen," Rob said. "Tell me how to activate the booth and I won't shoot."

"Fire on one of us," Dave said, "and you won't have time to react before the other two of us ruin your day."

"Don't be stupid, Whyte," Kevin said. "We could both make a lot of money. You *need* me."

"So does my wife, apparently," Rob said, with a touch of sad sarcasm.

Suddenly, a new set of feet could be heard coming down the stairs.

Rob felt something hard against the back of his heel. A small bump.

Sparky tore into the room.

BARK-BARK-BARK-BARK-BARK!

Rob's kidnappers turned to ward off the Lab-Basset, who was clearly in buzz-saw mode. The shotguns came up, aimed away from Rob.

Dr. Whyte made an instant decision. Raising his heel, he aimed his pistol at the largish computer tower sitting on the desk—the one that ran the software for Kevin's booth.

Timing, timing!

"Sorry Sparky," Rob said mournfully.

—Heel down on the bump, CLICK.

—Trigger pull, BANG!

Two actions, one instant.

In the tiniest fraction of a second it took for the bullet to exit the muzzle of the Beretta and bury itself into the hard drive of the computer tower, the booth flicked Rob from the basement of Kevin's lair to … what appeared to be someone's garage.

Again, an invisible force threw Rob around the booth. This time even more violently than before.

Rob stood up and stumbled out, pistol aimed back the way he'd come, prepared for whoever decided to follow.

When five minutes passed with no one coming to get him, Rob traced the second booth's cables to the second workstation, which he promptly shut down and unplugged, just for good measure.

Then he searched the house for a phone.

Then … he dialed the back line for Lightspeed Labs.

"You didn't call the police?" Jerryberry said incredulously. "Why didn't you call the police?"

"It would have been a mess trying to explain things to them right there in Kevin's living room. I was sure they'd have busted me for unlawful entry. The booths weren't part of the culture then, like they are now. They were a technological toy, and not entirely proven to work. A toy the legal system wasn't prepared for. Yet. So my first concern was with JumpShift. I had to let them know that I was not only alive, but well. And that we had a rather severe technical problem that had to be overcome before we could take the booths to market."

"So you *never* told the authorities?"

"In time, sure. Once everyone at Lightspeed Labs calmed down, and I'd been able to quietly exit Kevin's place—turned out he had a house within blocks of mine, where Daniella lived."

"Your wife. Right. What happened to her?"

"I divorced her."

"That's all?"

"What else could I do? There was no proof of anything. Just what Kevin had told me. And once I confronted Daniella about the affair—no mention of insurance or potential murder, just the affair—she quietly conceded. And agreed to an amicable split. Last I heard she'd been married twice more herself, though I think she died alone."

Jerryberry noticed that Rob's expression was sad, instead of vindictive. Though Daniella had clearly destroyed the marriage, some thread of affection still lingered in the old man's heart.

"Amazing," Jerryberry said.

"Want to know what else? They never did find Kevin or his buddies."

"Never?"

"Nope. Nevada state patrol eventually sent a chopper out to check that property, once I helped them zero in on it using an internet map. They found evidence of temporary habitation, and the wreck of Kevin's booth. But no people."

"So Kevin made it out alive?"

"Who knows? Personally, I think he and his three pals bit the dust. Dead within a day, in that heat, with no water. They couldn't stay at the house for fear that the fuzz would show up. So they tried to walk out—and never made it."

"You can't be sure," Jerryberry said.

"Nope. But when nobody tried to put a bullet in me or blow up my car within the first year after JumpShift's stock hit the market—and soared—I figured the window of real danger had passed. And I am reasonably certain that, all this time later, I was right in that assumption. But I never wanted to stir the hornet's nest, either. Which is why I've not gone public about the whole thing until you talked me into doing this exposé. Now that the project is almost ready to air, I can come clean."

"Did you ever feel bad?" Jerryberry asked.

"About what? Kevin? Not really. Like I said, we had a falling out when Daniella came around. Kevin was just as hot for her as I was. He didn't like that she took more of an interest in me, out of college, than him. So of course it probably felt like justice that he got to screw Daniella behind my back. In hindsight I think they deserved each other. I married Paula three years after the divorce from Daniella, got divorced again six years after that, and didn't meet Karolyn until JumpShift had made me a mega-millionaire."

"That sort of puts the lie to the idea that rich men can't find true love."

"Only because Karolyn and I had been friends in high school, and when the twenty-five-year reunion came around … well, anyway, she was divorced, I was divorced, we got to talking, and so forth. It was a quiet romance. Which was just fine by me, since JumpShift was giving me more public attention than I wanted, or could handle. Karolyn was like an island of calm amidst the publicity storm."

"Speaking of which, how did you fix the security hole, with the booths?"

"We encrypted the booth-to-booth signal that each of the booths uses to synchronize. Dumb and simple, really. Not nearly as mysterious or hard as Kevin made it sound. We'd have thought of it eventually, because the problem would have become apparent sooner or later. Kevin just rushed it to the forefront. Nowadays it's an afterthought, and the only way the different booth networks in the different countries can stay sorted out from each other. If your particular booth on your street corner can't 'talk' to the booth on the other side of town, then there's no flicking between them. Easy-peasy."

"Nice to know we've been protected all this time."

"It'd be major news before now, if you weren't. Bigger news than something like the mall riot, which exposed a different hole."

"Indeed," Jerryberry said. "Anyway, what I really meant to ask you was, did you ever feel bad about the *dog*?"

"Sparky? Oh, he lived to a ripe old age."

"But you said—"

"I saw Dave and Mike raise their guns, I never saw them fire."

"But how—"

"He was hungry as death when the Nevada cops showed up at the house, but he'd been drinking out of the toilet all week, so there wasn't any lasting harm done. I suppose maybe my one and only shot at the computer had diverted Kevin's boys' attention from Sparky? Or maybe they couldn't bring themselves to kill an innocent animal. Who knows? I do know that Sparky came home to me and stayed there, and fathered a nice bunch of puppies. I always did like that damned dog."

"Perfect," Jerryberry said, smiling.

He stood up from the chair and stretched, then went to the digital recorder and pressed the switch that turned it off. The little blue light grew dim, and darkened.

"You'll want to see my edited second run of this," Jerryberry said.

"Sure," Rob said, blinking his weary eyes.

Jerryberry pulled out his phone and checked the time.

"It's late. I'll start cutting this into the exposé tomorrow. The hidden story behind one of JumpShift's most potentially fatal foul-ups, narrowly averted by the quick thinking of JumpShift's founder."

"The dog did it," Rob said. "It was Sparky. If he'd not started making a racket when Kevin and his boys came back to the house, I'd have still been quietly fiddling with that inner door when they caught me. Probably would have died, right then. And now Kevin would be laying here in this bed, instead of me. Telling you his side of how it all worked out."

Jerryberry chuckled as he collapsed the tripod and packed his things.

"My alternate self is doing just that right now," he said.

Robin Whyte chuckled too.

"And my alternate self is snowboarding in Alaska."

"One can hope, Rob. Thanks for having me over for one more startling interview. As a newstaper, I could not have asked for anything better."

Rob's mouth suddenly stretched wide with a yawn. He coughed a couple of times, then wiped at his lower lip and looked up into Jerryberry's eyes—a pleading expression on the old man's face.

"Just make sure the exposé does me justice? More than that, make sure the exposé does JumpShift justice. We're a good company, Barry. Always have been. We ran it straight and we kept it narrow. We never gouged on price, and we always tried to deliver quality product with quality service. Not everyone appreciates that. Not everyone likes how we changed the world."

"Not even me, if I remember correctly," Jerryberry admitted.

"No, not even you."

The two men stared at each other for a moment.

"Goodnight, Rob," Jerryberry said, turning to go for the door.

"Goodnight, Barry," came the reply.

Jerryberry clicked off the light to the bedroom as he left. Dr. Whyte was already snoring.

A booth at the building's lobby took Jerryberry out.

He flicked four times, through four different quick snatches of scenery, then found himself back in the studio. A place he'd built with his own hands and money, until it had become one of the more respected color journalism newstaper offices in America.

Most everyone else had gone home, but Jerryberry was eager to work. If Rob had been right, there wasn't a lot of time left. And Jerryberry felt like he owed it to the old man to deliver him a finished product.

INTRODUCING
MATTHEW JOSEPH HARRINGTON

I first encountered Matthew Joseph Harrington when he wrote a story for the Man-Kzin Wars, of which I am an editor. In fact, he wrote several, all involving a protector. Protectors are part of my Known Space universe: they're the adult form of humanity and its progenitors, the Pak. The Pak breeder stage wasn't evolved for intelligence. The protector stage is a genius and a weapon.

If I'd caught him in time, I would have warned Matthew that writing about a character more intelligent than the author is the most difficult challenge he can face. Matthew didn't need the warning. Peace Corbin the human protector is a wonderful invention.

We knew each other pretty well when Matthew suggested collaboration. I did an easy thing: I sent him a partly finished novel that had gone stale on me, and hoped he'd get inspired. He did: he blitzed the rest of it, and we published the result as THE GOLIATH STONE in 2013.

When Michael suggested this book, Matthew was an obvious choice for inclusion.

Larry Niven

BOOK FOUR:
DISPLACEMENT ACTIVITY

MATTHEW JOSEPH HARRINGTON

GREG CAME INTO THE WATCHROOM to find Mike screening another of his weird vintage movies. This one was odder than usual, and that was saying something. What looked like a fairly pureblooded Oriental and a mixed African were beating each other up and wrecking the furniture in the process, which was not unusual for the era, but the dialogue decidedly was:

"Spartan dog!" Smash. "Roman cow!" Smash. "Spanish fly!" Smash. "Turkish Taffy!" Smash.

"What in hell are you watching?" Greg said.

Mike, normally quite the talker, looked at him, opened his mouth, looked at the screen, looked at Greg again, and said, "It's kind of hard to explain."

The lights dimmed.

At the Mercury Interstellar Receiving Station, the lights had *never* gone dim. Something had just come in with a phenomenal load of kinetic energy to dump. They both looked through the observation window at the arrival platform, imagining that the *Lazarus* rescue team had somehow rigged the derelict starship to self-transmit.

What they saw was a single man in a heavy armored suit, getting to his feet.

Check: not a man. His arms and legs were too long for his torso, though he did have the standard five-point body form that evolution favored on Earth ... and, apparently, wherever he was from too.

The alien turned slowly until he saw the window, and did something to his helmet—probably zooming in on them. He looked around again, visibly slumped, and did something to a forearm readout. Then he was gone again.

After an unknown amount of silence, Greg turned to Mike again and said, "Compared to what?"

Mike said, "We should send a report."

"Ya *think?*"

*****

The recording of the arrival created a great deal of excitement at the emergency JumpShift board meeting, as well it might. This was bigger than the discovery of *Lazarus*, and almost as big as teleportation itself. Back when the UN was still an expensive debating society, the Russian spy service had once come up with a transmitter small enough for a man to carry, but only to a dedicated receiver, and it didn't send the device along. (It hadn't worked out well for them; the first time an agent had used one, the people after him had promptly used the same thing to transmit a box of plastique to the same destination. Later models had a timed self-destruct built in, which had the effect of allowing an armed and accurate pursuer to blow up the agent carrying the thing. A plausible argument could be made that JumpShift had done less to bring down the Soviet Empire by breaking its isolation than by destroying KGB morale.)

The alien suit was clearly a self-transmitter, and obviously not tuned to a particular receiver. Director Bartholomew Jansen watched the recording less than halfway through before saying, "It's a lifeboat. Look at the legs. Scorch marks. Something went badly wrong for that guy, and he was trying to get home. I wonder how he missed?" He brushed his hand over the fringe of his snowy mountain-man beard as if it were a bubble he was trying not to pop, something he did when he was upset; his friends were of the view that he had too much empathy to be good for him.

Everyone else leaned forward to see that played back. Director Gail Strong, white hair coming in blonde again, said quietly, "I wonder where he'll end up." She and Jansen exchanged a glance. JumpShift had never made the mistake of giving top hire-and-fire authority to nontalent, but these two were talent without any technical knowledge.

Strong had come up with the continuous-teleport vacuum distillery—while dead drunk, at the party right after the transfer effect was first achieved—and had been kept on salary for over sixty years since, in the hope that she would come up with something else as lucrative. Last year, when Jump-Shift was sued by an Oregon sect whose members claimed that using transfer booths had removed their souls, she had persuaded the judge to have the plaintiffs watch *Old Yeller* in court. The jury was back in about twenty minutes. Worth every penny.

Jansen had suggested the Riot Control system for dealing with flash mobs. After that, Robin Whyte had, essentially, backed progressively larger truckloads of money up to his house until he agreed to join the Board. A couple of years after that, Jansen had thought up the notion of putting an east-west divider inside distillery towers, up to just a little below the level of the seawater inside, and painting the side facing the Equator black. That way water would heat up and evaporate faster on the sunny side of the tower, sink due to higher salt content, and refill from the shady side. JumpShift hadn't needed a tower cleaned out or equipped with circulation pumps since.

Discussion among the other Board members was brisk at first, largely concerning how a self-transmitter could be made so small and still send itself, with equally excitable remarks about a power supply that could do repeat jumps. It gradually died down as people noticed that the two nontechnical Members, who had increased net company profits more than the rest of them put together, weren't talking to anyone but each other.

Chairman Boynton said, "Any ideas from the Advising Directors?"

Jansen said, "We were wondering how long it takes a body in transit to lose a definable position from interaction with matter."

Samuel Watt, who had recently retired from heading Engineering, said, "A body in transit doesn't interact with matter."

"Bullshit," said Strong cheerfully. (The Kurtzberg-Simon treatments were doing a wonderful job of improving cell-wall function, but a side effect of the resulting rejuvenation was that it tended to make the patient somewhat aggressive.) "It interacts with the receiver just fine, or we wouldn't have a business—except selling garbage disposals."

"And getting rid of bodies," Jansen murmured. He'd been a newsman once. It had never entirely worn off.

Watt stared at them hard and raised an arthritis-knotted finger, but nothing came out of his mouth for a while. Then he said, "So you're wondering if someone who's in transit long enough could be picked up just anywhere, right?"

"Right," said Jansen, and Strong gave Watt a big smile.

"I am goddamned if I know. I'm not even sure how to check in a single lifetime."

"Why does it have to be in a single lifetime?" Strong said. "We were thinking it might be a good idea to build a refuge. Someplace where lost travelers can be collected and provided with a habitable environment."

"And their technology studied?" said Watt.

"Why not?"

The discussion went on for another hour, but the final decision, to start building, was unanimous. Details would accumulate, but the feeling was that it would ultimately be the least trouble to build it about as far out as the orbit of Xuxa, though not near the planet itself. There was plenty of material in the cometary halo, and it could be delivered to the worksite by teleportation without worrying about velocity and temperature changes. Not worrying much, anyway.

Watt had spent most of the discussion doing work on his computer. After the meeting, he caught up with Strong and said, "I've got a WAG on the dispersal figure. I based it on the effective limit of a single standard launch laser, which disperses to resemble inverse-square illumination after about twelve lightyears, and worked in a fudge factor based on the interaction rate of the highest-frequency neutrinos—" At this point he took notice of her corpselike patience and skipped a lot of stuff. "It looks like maybe twenty thousand years. Could be wrong by a factor of two, either way. Could also be blowing smoke. But if it's right, someone who departed from the Galactic core fifty thousand years back could, today, arrive just about anywhere in the Galaxy."

"There wouldn't be any single place likelier than another?"

"Nope. Anywhere within the lightspeed radius would be just as probable as anywhere else. In fact, based on some of Hawking's work, possibly a little outside the lightspeed radius too. Technically it'd be faster-than-light travel."

Strong blinked, slowly. "Do you mean to say you could send a message to Andromeda, get into a transfer booth, and arrive before the message did?"

Watt shook his head as if trying to dislodge a horsefly from his middle ear—which, with his bony face and long gray hair, was disturbing on a number of levels. "*No,*" he said, visibly irritated. "Intergalactic matter is too thin. There has to be enough material to disperse the signal. The effect would be strictly local."

"Local meaning only within your own galaxy," Strong said, deadpan.

"Right," said Watt, who either didn't get the joke or had meant that in the first place.

Strong had seen engineers when they were in work mode, and moved on. "I'm wondering if we should provide Mercury with more people. And maybe weapons."

Watt said, "Well, the argument that they can get more people there fast enough to have to pay for the pizza still applies." They exchanged a grin. Nobody younger than they were would have gotten the joke, of course. "And if some unpleasant stranger arrives with something that can be used faster than they can hit the Retransmit button, having weapons around won't do anything much except increase the chance of an accident. I'm a little concerned that somebody nonhuman will be cooled to the wrong temperature. I wish Whyte had done some basic research on that; I'm not sure anyone else ever had the brains to figure out why it is that an inertial-compensation receiver doesn't automatically chill a cargo to absolute zero. Hell, I'm not satisfied about why it's never reversed left for right!"

"The left-right thing I know," she said. "Robin said the transition particle has the internal structure of whatever you transmit. And I remember that had something to do with how he figured out how to do compensation. He realized the original booths had to be doing a little momentum compensation anyway, because you always arrive oriented to the floor of the booth, but no two booth floors on Earth would be in exactly the same plane. Every time you transfer, you rotate a little in whatever direction you're going, but we never tipped over a wedding cake—sorry, I think I'm having another contaminant dump." (The projected lifespan of someone who'd had a full course of KS treatments was around 170 years, at which time cell division was expected to peter out. The sudden bursts of increased alertness and vitality were still catching her by surprise.)

"It's a damned shame Whyte didn't live long enough to get that stuff," Watt said. "How the hell do we know he was right about transition particle structure? It's not something we can check. You know, it's entirely possible he just hit it lucky. There may be aliens out there who never developed transfer technology because they tried a system that doesn't require a booth to be a transceiver, so transmitter and receiver didn't automatically have identical circuit structure, and there was a huge antimatter explosion that wrecked their civilization."

"Bite your tongue. Robin used to have nightmares about that when he was working on it."

"I just bet he did."

"So, when we've got a ship ready to go, you'll be looking in on the work?"

Watt looked aghast. "Hell, no. I'm not going there until the receiver's built. Space travel is *dangerous*."

*****

As Samuel Watt stepped into the booth, he reflected, not for the first time, that he should either send a proxy to Board meetings for him or stop getting distracted by engineering concerns. He hadn't been paying close enough attention to the details of the planning session. The ship sent out was a prototype that had been under construction, which some smart aleck had christened the *Norman Dean*. It used the same reaction mass over and over, continuously transmitting it from the tail to the nose and running it through a central accelerator, and it had a whopping big additional transceiver built into the cargo section already, for everything else. The ship's acceleration meant that the mass arriving in the nose receiver was cooler than when it was transmitted. However, the point was not to build up a huge reaction speed relative to the ship, but to save weight on the ship; and since the reaction mass, of incandescent plasma, was *inside the ship*, the fact that it never heated up past a certain point didn't bother the crew one little bit.

It did mean that Watt would end up commuting to the goddamn ship for progress sessions.

The color of the booth wall changed, and he was out past the orbit of Jupiter: he bounced into the air a little, under his own muscle tension. When the booth opened, the engineer on monitor duty greeted him with, "Welcome aboard our bucket."

Watt had to smile at that. Sooner or later every ship was called a bucket by its crew, but the *Norman Dean* really was one: the bow was an open-ended cylinder with a transmitter in constant operation, sending stuff to a similar receiver at the stern. Friction with ambient material was close to zero. "Hi," he said, reaching her in one long low-G lope. "Sam Watt." He waited for her to make the obligatory, "Sam what?" joke.

"Theresa Joule," she replied. "*Not* 'Terry.'" Her freckles weren't noticeable until she scowled.

"I am never complaining about my name again," he said. (He never did, either. Whatever were her parents thinking?) "Since I'm here, I gather things are going well?"

"Operational," she said. "I've been playing with some ideas, though."

At 74, Watt was still not immune to the mixture of interest and alarm that occurred when a younger member of his profession said that. "So what you got?"

She took a display flat and punched up a circuit diagram. "I got to thinking about the old Soviet version of the transfer booth. There's three different places in a transceiver where a frequency generator is used. The Soviets set this one," she pointed, "to a different wavelength, and Soviet transceivers couldn't connect up with JumpShift's. Supposed to prevent defections. Of course, the CIA immediately told all their best tech people how to alter theirs to send to our kind of booth, and put receivers on ships in the Indian Ocean. Anyway, the thing is, theirs used a little more power because the internal signal is less …" She gestured, trying to find the right word.

"Coherent."

"Yes, thank you! I've been doing simulations, putting in different values for these circuit modules, and there are other settings that are about as good as ours. They're just as coherent, just different. With circuit elements like humans use, JumpShift's circuit generates the transfer effect faster than the others, but look at this." She fiddled with the image and replaced transistors with vacuum tubes. "Now, this setting uses more power—"

"But it gets the signal out even faster once the tubes are warmed up!" he saw at once. "And compensation will be a lot easier, too."

"And transistors aren't exactly an obvious idea."

"Hell, no. You realize this means we'll have to build two big transceivers instead of one."

"There's room," she said. She frowned. "That's the only part that bugs me about this. It's so empty out there."

"True. On the other hand, if the Sun blows up we'll be in an unrivaled position to say, 'What was that?'"

"Oh, that's true," she said, cheering up.

Engineers. You had to love them. (The alternative was strangling them, and he didn't want that catching on.)

There had been something Strong said at the Board meeting, and he'd let it go by at the time, but it had started preying on his mind since. "We need to make them a lot bigger than originally planned, too."

She nodded. "You'd better talk to Captain Philips."

JumpShift had revolutionized spaceships even before the *Norman Dean*—the lack of a need for on-site recycling, or even baggage aside from a single change of clothing, was a godsend—but this bucket was really something. Reuse of the same reaction mass meant constant acceleration, but the acceleration was tiny. In principle, you could climb a ladder with two fingers. (In practice, when you do that you keep whacking your knuckles on the next rung you reach for, and he soon quit fooling around.)

The skipper had just finished low-G calisthenics, indicating he was not one of those people naturally immune to bone loss, and therefore must have been enormously more capable than every applicant who was. He was just vacuuming a layer of sweat off when they were admitted to the foyer of his quarters. (The *ND* was roomy, too. Why not?)

He gave Watt an instant of searingly undivided attention, nodded, inspected his own right hand, vacuumed it a little more, and held it out to shake. "Pleased to meet you, Dr. Watt."

"Sam."

"Ralph. Describe your needs and I'll see what I can do." He pulled on a sweatsuit as Watt spoke.

"We'll need to build at least two receivers." He explained about the other possible circuits.

"Doable," said Ralph. "Plenty of supplies out there. Might not get much we can use from the technology of the vacuum-tube folks. Be interesting to look at, though."

"Also, one possibility that was suggested at the meeting that started this mission was that somebody out there might have figured out how to build a transmitter, but not a receiver—"

"So when we switch on our general receiver, it immediately explodes from the arrival of a thousand-year planetary supply of smelter slag and bargain-brand toy knockoffs. I see."

"I was thinking more like eggshells, coffee grounds, and orange peels."

"A civilization that doesn't compost those doesn't last any thousand years," Ralph said.

"They could get more material from the cometary halo. We had rockets long before transfer booths."

"And it'd be in simple molecules, too, good point." Ralph was a pleasure to talk with. Got it in one. "That's not good. We'll have to make each one in the form of a long tube, and run the receiver activation pulse down it at high speed."

"I was thinking of just making a very big box."

"No way of knowing in advance if it was big enough. With a pulsed tube we can get stuff in installments. Also, using it for something as simplistic as garbage disposal is a very top-down approach, so it's likely to be a society that has political prisoners. Way easier to rescue them from a tube. Put in lots of access hatches." Ralph paused to study Sam, frowned slightly, took him by the arms, turned him over, and held him by the ankles. "You were going into shock," he said before Sam could ask. "Easiest way to get blood back to your brain."

"I was just thinking, thank God the Soviet engineers never told their bosses that the only reason for the cable network is to turn on the right receiver."

Ralph turned Sam up again, raised his eyebrows—to considerable effect; the man must have more sheer personality than a cat—and said, "Wait a minute. You mean, all that time, the Party thought people were being transported as *energy*, over what amounted to *telephone wires?*"

"If you can think of another reason why they kept the gulags open instead of exiling people to nowhere, I'm listening."

Ralph's eyes got even bigger than they had been, and he looked like he was trying not to laugh. "And they never promoted anybody who could do the math, because anyone who could do enough math to understand physical limits would be opposed to socialism in the first place. And those guys popped out as soon as they knew how anyway. Right. Okay. Let's—" Abruptly he pressed a fist to his mouth, closed his eyes tightly, made a strangled noise, and shook very hard for a moment. Then he relaxed and said, "Sorry. Let's sign you in and get started. You'll need to pick a password."

Ralph's swift grasp of the implications, so thorough that he'd found the needle of humor in a haystack of nightmare, was not a fluke. His level of competence was such that he had something useful to say about every aspect of the designs. Four hours along, with the basics hammered out, he did a final save, shut off the tabletop screen they were using, and said, "My eyes are peeled onions. We should start with the standard one, and we can use it to make vacuum tubes on the spot." He chuckled and shook his head. "There's just something about my family and tubes."

Dots connected in Sam's brain. "Philips Cryogenic!" he said. It was a patent JumpShift had missed: build a sealed tower, at the South Pole to avoid lateral drift from Coriolis force, and use uncompensated transceivers to send things from the bottom to the top, over and over, until they were as cold as you wanted, then use a compensated receiver to catch the mass. Philips had cornered the market on liquefied gases the week they started up. A similar process in vacuum also worked to separate isotopes; but, as a few Third World nations had learned when they tried to take the nuclear shortcut to move up in the rankings, not only was quality control a fussy thing, but lateral drift *really mattered*. Their successor governments had devoted more attention to things like resource development. And disaster relief.

Ralph blinked at him. "You didn't know that? Yeah, I'm named for my great-grandfather. You should meet him."

"He's still alive?"

"Barring a direct meteor strike since I called him last, yeah. He's one of those people who kind of seasons with age, like Cohen the Barbarian. Quit the CIA to start the company when he had the idea. Hasn't done a day's work since."

"Why do you?"

"Who says I'm working? I like flying spaceships."

Samuel Watt was not equipped to agree with the specific choice, but the attitude was one he shared. "Beats freezing people for a living," he said.

"Ralph the Great—uh, family nickname—says that's going to peter out since the alien showed up. He's already planning to offer terminal patients a trip to the future *sans* freezing. Even with KS treatments, it's got to be kind of hard to cure a disease if the patient's already dead." Ralph paused and frowned at him.

"Don't turn me over again, okay? Jesus, I never even imagined that. He's right. In twenty thousand years we ought to have a cure for anything we can even describe today."

"Not necessarily. If sick people get themselves sent to nowhere, what's the motivation for finding cures? He just thinks they'll find it a lot cheaper than slow death and funeral expenses. He's an awful cynic, but I see his point. Why ruin your family?"

Sam saw the calm logic of it, but shook his head. "Motivation doesn't enter into it. Fleming discovered penicillin because he couldn't afford an assistant to keep his lab sterile. Sulfas came out of the *fabric dye* industry, for pity's sake. And people working on problems teleportation can't help with discover stuff all the time. Like the people working on things like nanomachinery for construction. Why not constructing healthy bodies?"

Ralph half-smiled. "Real Soon Now," he said, a catch-word among engineers, referring in this case to the fact that working nanotech had been predicted as "fifty years away" when transfer booths had been invented, and was still so described. At least they weren't losing any ground.

"Maybe not. But in twenty thousand years? Random other stuff. Hell, the KS treatments were originally intended as a preparation for dying people who planned to be frozen, to keep their cells from bursting! Then they gave 'em to somebody who was dying of plain old age, and lo and behold, he got up."

"I know, okay? Ralph the Great gave us all chapter and verse last Fourth of July, when he started taking them. Scary how much better they make everything work, too. Nevada casinos won't let him in now. Caught him counting off an eight-deck shoe. I live in dread of the day he studies piloting. He'll show up here, I know it."

"Suggest Monte Carlo. They're up to twenty decks now."

Ralph looked startled, then produced a wider smile than his face ought to have held without the top of his head coming off. "I will, thanks. Even if he can do it, they'll never believe it." He stretched, got a bottle of water, drank it off like Thor in Jotunheim, and said, "I'll copy what we've got to Theresa."

"She a good engineer?"

"Anybody ever ask you to run a reactionless spaceship?"

After Sam thought it over, "My goodness," was all he could say at first. Once the file was sent, he asked, "Has she seen the footage of the alien's arrival?"

"Sure, we all did."

"If she's the best, I'd be interested in hearing her ideas on what our visitor was using for a power supply. We've been going nuts. Nobody's ever built a self-transmitter smaller than a Phoenix hull that wasn't a one-shot."

"What did the KGB use for the spy cloak?"

"Cesium-fluorine power cell."

Ralph's eyes got bigger than they'd been so far. "You'd never get me into one of those things. Hell, I wouldn't stand *next* to someone *carrying* one of those things."

"Yah."

She'd been working on the power source problem. For fun.

"It's the Bacardi reaction. Got to be. Protons and lithium." This was named for the original Cockcroft-Walton experiment, which produced 151 times as much energy as it took to accomplish.

It wasn't in use for power plants, because there was a problem: "Lithium's awfully fussy to work with," Sam said. "How about proton-boron-beryllium?"

She shook her head. "Limit to how small you can make the shielding. And beryllium's hellishly poisonous stuff even if you catch all the neutrons coming off. And you have to clean out the carbon waste—"

"But stray alpha is helium and comes out on its own, I got it. That it on his back?" They had the record running in a loop.

"Nope." She grinned. "That's his recycler. The power source is on that belly plate. See how it gives off some IR just before he goes?"

"That recycler's *tiny*."

"Don't be too impressed. Probably just air and water. I doubt he's supposed to use it very long."

"Oh, good point." He'd expected to get home immediately, of course.

"That power plant is smaller than we could build, though," she said. "If I had an unlimited budget I might be able to fit one into a motorcycle fridge. Might not. I would *really* like to see the insides of that thing."

"How big is a motorcycle fridge?" He'd never even heard of them.

She held up her hands to indicate opposing corners of a cube about ten inches on a side. "Runs off the engine. You've never been club camping? Everybody brings one thing."

"Never." It sounded like one of those sneaky ways to teach kids survival and organizational skills, like the Boy Scouts, which he'd left under a cloud after bringing a "snipe" back to camp. (It had been black with a couple of white stripes. Quite peaceful, too, before all the yelling. Ambled into the sack on its own while his eyes were shut, or he'd have had a clue.)

"Really lets you know who you can rely on," she went on, unthinkingly confirming his notion.

"...!" said Sam, utterly unable to recall what he'd been about to say due to an absolutely terrific crick in the left side of his neck, from looking down at the plans for so long. It ran about halfway down his arm, which he grabbed and began to massage.

"Well, shit," said Theresa in the most reasonable of conversational tones. She grabbed him by his right arm, put him into the small-cargo booth, and said, "There's always a stand-by team for medical emergencies." Then she shut the door and bounded to her console.

Nothing changed until the booth opened to reveal Theresa, now drenched with sweat and accompanied by the sound of an alarm. "Son of a *bitch*!" She slapped a switch nearby and said, "Captain, he's back. Receivers on Earth must be offline."

"Jesus, of course they are," said Ralph's voice. "Damn. Get him into a survival bubble. We're about to have a proof of concept."

"Captain, we can't!" she said, but broke a pack off the wall as she spoke. She pulled the inflation pin.

"It's that or let him die. We don't have anything for a heart attack here. The first ten minutes are critical."

"I'm getting a pain patch on him," she said, slapping one on Sam's neck. "That'll give me time to write on the label." She stuffed Sam into the bubble and wrote something on the lid in big block letters.

Sam had narcotics being distributed through his Circle of Willis by then, or he'd have been able to say, "It's a muscle spasm. I've *had* a heart attack. My heart's a cultured replacement."

Theresa's eyes were sheened with unspilled tears when she said, "I'm sorry, Doc. It's the only way." She sealed the bubble, then he heard her shut the booth.

*****

He was in free fall, it was dark, and things were banging on the outside of the bubble.

And everybody he knew was dead.

Abruptly his left side slammed against the inside of the bubble. He was just getting used to the concept of that being "down" when the pull changed and the bubble whacked the top of his head.

He was scrabbling for a handhold (the Engineer who was most often in charge of his brain was noting that these goddamn things should have interior straps, padding, *and a light*) when the bubble opened and he saw someone uglier than he would have believed a human being could be.

He was right, too. This was an alien.

"You are safe," it enunciated with great precision, spraying him all over with what looked like a plant fogger. "I am an orderly. A kyuman doctor is nearby, on call. Do you need kelp?"

It was a design feature of emergency patches that they needed a specific solvent to remove. That kept a patient, who might have been, say, concussed, suicidal, or just stupid, from taking them off. Regrettably, in the present circumstances, just such a patch, designed to keep an angina victim from dying of traumatic shock, was hosing down the brain of someone who merely had a neck cramp, who was being questioned by an alien whose soft palate evidently had no middle position, which caused it to sound like a really dedicated holistic practitioner.

It would be some little while later before Samuel Watt was able to articulate this, even to himself. Meanwhile, with an act of will bordering on the superhuman, he reached up to touch the patch on his neck, then tapped his head.

"You are stoned? I will assist you." Very long arms reached into the bubble, under his arms, and lifted him out. As it sprayed the rest of him, the alien said, "Your shell label says your problem is a cart attack. We get a lot of those, but usually after they arrive. No?"

Sam had been shaking his head. He tapped his chest, then tried to hold up both thumbs, but only succeeded in some mild thrashing. (His real heart attack had not only given him a tolerance for narcotics, it had made him something of a connoisseur, and whatever this stuff was, it had definitely not been on the menu back then. Wow.)

"You may be in error." The alien moved him to a seat, pulled a belt across his lap—there was *some* gravity, more than the ship's thrust, but still not much—and pulled up his shirt. The scar was conspicuous, and the alien said, "New?"

Sam nodded.

"There could still be a problem." It pulled something like a fat stethoscope out of a nearby table-mounted box and pressed the end to his chest, where it stayed, connecting him to the box. The alien looked at the box, whose inside cover now showed a remarkably clear image of a beating heart, with nine rows of jiggling lines underneath. Sam decided it might be a separate line for each chamber of the heart, and a function readout for each lobe of the lungs. "Kealthy. Well, that is. Better than mine. Muscle spasm caused a false alarm?" Sam nodded. "That is rare and sad. I will call a counselor for orientation." It turned to a wall console and began tapping colored spaces.

Sam, who was drying out fast, looked around and saw a thoroughly ordinary examining room, with the usual cabinets, drawers, sink, and even a frosted-glass window in the door. He was sure this was a deliberate attempt to be reassuring. There must be a hell of a lot of people from around his time.

He was moderately distressed to see narrow black stains along most of the corners where walls came together. It bespoke a breakdown in maintenance procedures.

The alien wore coveralls in pale gray, and had what seemed to be the same proportions as the alien in the film from Mercury Station, but the resemblance to humans went very little further. Its skin was dusty orange. The orifice it talked with was almost between two widely-set nearly-human eyes, and Sam tentatively tagged the cashew-shaped holes below the eyes as nostrils. If he was right, it could breathe while swallowing, a much better design than Earth vertebrates enjoyed. Ears could be the shallow bubbles on the sides of the head, and they were below jarringly normal-looking hair in a humanlike hairline. Brown and wavy. Better than Sam's, really.

Sam jumped a little when it reached over to the box it had opened, to get out a spray bottle, and he saw that the elbows were ball-and-socket joints. Harder to injure than hinge joints, but might not support as much weight.

The alien turned back to him, sprayed the patch, and removed it. The patch was carefully placed in a small plastic bag. "We save these," said the alien. "Some supplies are card to make quickly, and we are getting another cluster of arrivals lately, in excess of reserves. A counselor is on the way. I asked for a female just in case. We know about kyumans." It nodded a couple of times—that neck was all cables, no sign of a larynx—and added, "Can you talk yet?"

Sam made some foolish noises, shook his head, and pointed back and forth between his own throat and the alien's.

"Neck? Throat? Voice? My voice. It's at the back." It pointed well back on the side of its own neck, and nodded twice more. "You are observant. Not usually the first question. I'm sorry, I know your name. I am familiarly called Tolul, and I am male. This matters to us as well, but not in the same way as to you." Tolul nodded several more times. (Was that amusement?) He studied Sam's face, and Sam studied him back. Those irises weren't irises, they were internal lids that closed from the sides, with another set behind them that closed vertically. It looked like he could close his nostrils, too. Tolul nodded slightly and held up a hand to be inspected. It looked like a human hand, but with an extra thumb opposite the usual one, instead of a pinky. *Exactly* like one. "We're willing to make improvements," Tolul said. "Our natural cands are more obviously adapted paws than yours. I got mine fixed."

Somebody short showed up beyond the frosted glass of the door, and Tolul said, "Aa." The door opened, and Tolul said, "O. This is Davoost. She is in command kere."

Davoost was another alien, unquestionably a different species. She was about four feet tall, chunky, and what he could see of her skin was hairless and very pale, with darker blotches. If more of the blotches met up she'd have looked something like a bald miniature panda. She was, bluntly, cute.

Sam had never trusted cute. He had frequently been told this was an unreasoning prejudice.

The black body armor and the sidearm did nothing to disabuse him of his views.

"Does he work?" she said. At least her voice wasn't cute. She sounded like an angry bullfrog. (On reflection, Tolul's voice was as strange as his hair. He sounded very human, and oddly familiar.)

Tolul replied—sounding exactly like Davoost—"Key is not dying but will need kelp to stay sane. Key is the first. Samuel Watt."

"So?" she said.

"As in Samuel Watt Rescue Station."

The shock of realizing they'd named the place for him was slightly greater than abruptly figuring out that Tolul had been addressing him in his, Sam's, own voice. Sam was familiar with this as a calming technique; long ago, he'd used a delayed recording of himself to cure his snoring, and years later gave the playback system to his sister Judith, whose first baby refused to stop crying no matter what she did. (It only worked while the playback was on. The issue finally went away when a TV was put in her nursery. She'd been *bored*.)

The issue arose of how he could know what Sam's voice sounded like without hearing it first. Personal sonar to map his throat?

Davoost stared at Sam in a way that made him wonder if he was edible and hope he was poison. "You have respect here."

"Oh?"

"Can't breathe respect," she said. "Get sane so you can do work."

The door opened behind her, and she dropped her hand to her gun as she turned.

"Orientation," said the woman who came in. Sam stared. She carried a large bag, which he scarcely noticed: she was dressed in nothing but a push-up corset, a garter belt, fishnets, and stiletto heels, all brilliant red, which set off her wavy black hair and deep brown South Asian skin nicely. Her generous figure did *not* need the corset … but it didn't do any harm, either.

"This is Mr. Watt," said Tolul.

Sam found he could now form actual words in his mind, and thus probably in his mouth.

Okay, he thought, *I'm exiled to the future, bad shock, have to adapt, and the first three people I see are a Growleywog, a rabid stuffed toy, and a porn star who is evidently on duty.*

This place needs new management.

"Watt? Oh, then he's from Scotland! Hobbellobbo," said the woman. "Yobbou spobbeak obbEnglobbish?"

He hadn't heard it since high school. Insert the syllable "obb" before every spoken vowel sound, and place the accent on the "obb." Not secure from a bright teenaged speaker of English, but capable of driving the average public school teacher to issuing even more demented edicts than usual, which was the point. "Yobbes, obbI dobboo. Obbis thobbere trobbou-bobble?" (He'd always been proud of "trobboubobble.")

She gave him a bright smile. "Obboh yobbes," she said. "He needs sex quickly," she said.

Davoost made a belching noise. "Do that, then," she said. "And teach him the common language."

The woman said, "Wobbee nobbeed tobboo tobbalk," came over, leaned down, and kissed him at length.

Davoost belched again. "Not in public! Gross creatures!"

The woman undid his lap belt, straightened up, and said, "Dobbon't tobbake obbit obbout obbuntobbil obbI sobbay."

Sam nodded, wondering how she'd been able to speak around whatever it was she'd slipped into his mouth.

She took him by the hand and led him out of the examination room, and they were in a long, wide corridor, which looked like it might have been part of an absolutely typical 21st-century hospital, except that the floor curved up in the distance.

Rotational gravity, no wonder it was low. The gentler the curve, the faster the spin needed to be, and this place had to be miles across. Too much spin would put a strain on fullerite, let alone metal.

That mildew or whatever was visible in every interior edge he looked at carefully.

A human emergency team rushed past them, with a gurney bearing a human patient, who had either been exposed to vacuum or spent decades working on a rum-blossom worthy of a Surgeon-General. Almost all the people Sam saw were human, and most of the aliens were the gangly types. The cute ones were rare.

The cute ones were also all readily visible, because everyone went wide around them. Except the emergency team; every alien moved aside for that.

She took him to a room whose door had no window, closed it behind them, and said, "All right, it won't be a problem now. Chups and tols think humans are perverts because we don't have a mating season, so they never look into these rooms."

Sam wasn't surprised. He was still getting used to the decor.

The sex toys and bondage furniture actually didn't bother him quite as much as the fact that the red carpeting covered the floor, the walls, and the ceiling, except for one large mirror and the glowing white globes in the room's eight corners to provide the light. He finally decided that what the place looked like was a set from a film warning parents about their children having sex, said film having been directed by a monk who had been brooding on the topic for the past forty years.

"You can take it out now," she said.

Sam grunted and removed the thing from his mouth. It was an oblong gray plastic capsule, and looked like nothing much.

"No, no, you were supposed to swallow that. It's a tracking jammer. You thought I meant that?" She laughed, then grew serious. "You're not celibate, are you? It'll make it difficult to talk very often if you are."

"No, but I'm in my seventies." (Not counting transit time, of course.)

Her eyebrows rose and tried to come together. "So am I."

"I haven't had access to your kind of medicine."

"The restoratives should be starting to work by now."

"What restoratives?"

"The shots Tolul gave you."

"I never got any. We were interrupted by Davoost."

Her eyes widened in dismay, and she said, "Swallow that *right now.*"

Alarmed, he did so (not difficult, teflon coating), and she bent forward, tucked her shoulder into his belly, picked him up, opened the door, and ran into someone immediately. They all landed on the hall floor in a loose pile.

It was Tolul. "I calve to give you some treatments for your kealth," he said once he'd reached a sitting position. He produced a pressure injector, not so much a pistol as a small Tommy gun, complete with drum magazine. "I'm sorry I forgot. Please remove most of your clothing."

People were going past frequently. Sam, not sure whether he was supposed to let Tolul know he spoke something other than gibberish, pointed at the open door.

Tolul pulled his elbows in and held his hands before his neck. "I would rather not."

Okay, that was embarrassment or something like it. Sam couldn't blame him. He stood and took off his shirt, shoes, and pants. He then got very small shots in twenty-seven places. Individually, each was as easily ignored as a pinch. By the twenty-seventh pinch, however, Sam was in a mood such that if he was told, oops, he needed just one more, then whoever subsequently managed to pull his, Sam's, foot out of Tolul's butt would immediately become king of England.

Tolul said, "You will not get sick now," and patted Sam on top of his head, this being what he clearly knew from experience was just about the only place where Sam didn't have a fresh pinhole with a sore lump underneath.

Unfortunately it was where Sam had landed when being retrieved, so it hurt anyway. "Ow."

Tolul exposed teeth like a lamprey's, quickly covered his mouth with his free hand, and said, "Sorry. Kere." He hung the injector on his belt, got out a pill, and said, "Take this. Pain will stop soon."

Sam glanced at—he still didn't know her name—and got a slight smile, so he took it. She put a fingertip under his chin and led him back into the room, and Tolul departed without further comment.

"How do you feel?" she said.

Sam gave her an incredulous look. "How fast is it supposed—I will be dipped for a sheep. What is *in* those?" He was already improving.

"An isopiate bound to a prostaglandin counter, in a liquid osmosis facilitator. The capsule coating breaks down on contact with hydrogen chloride, which anyone in a lot of pain has plenty of in his stomach."

"An opiate? How much?" He'd seen addicts when he was a kid, before wireheading became legal and killed them all off.

"Damn little. The compound only breaks down where the tissue is damaged and releases the narcotic on the spot. I thought they had that in your time."

"Injected. I usually managed to stay out of hospitals. How's Earth doing?"

She stared at him. "You really are one of the very first sent, aren't you? Earth is charcoal. The Sun went giant."

Sam sat very carefully on the bed. *"How the hell long has it been?"*

She shook her head quickly. "Sixteen thousand years and change. Sol was expanding and contracting long before humans evolved, and the cycles were constantly getting shorter. In hindsight it was obvious it had a lot more waste material inside it than age could account for on its own. The current guess is that it's about a fourth-generation star. Born old, like a clone. For a long time people thought the extra heavy elements were necessary to produce life, but after we started getting tol and chup who knew some physics we learned different. They didn't have stars like that; just us."

"Tolul would be a tol?"

"Right. It's just a coincidence of names, like a human named 'Manny.' Mine's Marjorie Fein, what's yours, Mr. Watt?"

"Samuel."

She stared at him. Then she said, "Take the rest of your clothes off."

"Look, that's not necessary."

"To whom? I didn't get selected by lot, you know. The chup don't even approve of this job. Besides, you've just had a full course of restoratives. You're going to get heffened any minute."

"What's 'heffened' m—" Sam took a fast deep breath, let it out slowly, and took another. The sensation he was feeling was one he'd never thought could be duplicated: the one he'd felt when he was seventeen and doing extra work after school, and Ms. Zachau casually tossed her panties on his lab table on her way to the storage room.

"That," said Marjorie.

After some time—and it sure was some time—Marjorie said, "Questions, or sleep?"

As long days went, this had probably been the record, but—"I thought everybody was supposed to be beige in the future. Nobody I saw was. You look Indian."

She grinned. "You'd completely baffle anyone who wasn't in Orientation if you said that. The term you want is 'Guptani.' 'Indios' is a term first directly applied to people in the New World, long before India was called that by its own people. Originally 'Indios' was due to the error of location, then later it became a pun, because the people seemed to possess a strain of innocence that Europeans hadn't encountered before, and were regarded as closer to divinity: 'in dios.' In fact, they weren't all that innocent, just not up on all the scams. I'm afraid you're going to hear me being pedantic a lot. Orientation is fundamentally immersive teaching. You can choose what you look like, doesn't cost much. I chose a Guptani appearance after a lot of study of Earth's cultures. Many of them made sexuality into a religion or an art form, but only the Guptani made it into a philosophical study." She beamed at him. "I think it makes me sexier."

"So do I. Why hasn't the language changed?"

"It did, for a while. Almost all my ancestors were from ships that were in transit during the Evacuation, and they either came here or someone went and got them. By the time the human refugees started to show up in the tube, nobody here could understand them, but the chup said everybody had to learn one language, and there were a lot more refugees than locals, so we all ended up speaking your kind of American, more or less. Most useful language in history."

"Human history." You didn't last long as an engineer if fanatical nitpicking wasn't a reflex.

"Any history. The chup and the tol both had rigid formal rules of language. Very old cultures. American used to be called 'English' before it got complicated. English got started on an island that used to get invaded every few generations by new strangers, and people really had to work to make themselves understood. So far it's been able to express any thought anybody can form—sometimes because, if it doesn't have a word for something, it steals one and blanks the chip ID."

That sounded like the modern equivalent of filing off the serial numbers. Fair enough. "Oh. So 'heffening' is from an alien word?"

She frowned. "No, human, and from about your time I think. Regular verb, artificial origin I believe, 'causing arousal and heightened esthetic perception to an unexpected and pleasing degree.' I heffen, you heffen—"

Light dawned and Sam interrupted. "*Ah* ha. I get it. Derived from 'heffener.'"

"That was a word already?"

"A name." It was a shame the man hadn't lived to hear he'd been verbed. "Good term for it. What was in those shots, anyway?"

"Twenty-five targeted retroviruses for repairing chromosomes and mitochondrial DNA, the KSP treatment, and enough ATP to get it all started. Men need one more shot than women so the Y chromosome isn't ignored. It's the price you pay for being taller and stronger." She smiled.

"That and zippers," Sam said. "Not worried about infectious diseases?"

"No, the KSP covers that."

The term suddenly registered. "It used to be 'KS.' Does 'P' stand for 'Philips'?"

"Yes, when he was starting the refuge Captain Philips turned out to be something of a heinlein."

Sam absorbed that, nodding. "Almost everybody I've seen was human. Earth was evacuated, got it. The aliens aren't refugees?"

Marjorie looked glum. "Most residents here were born here, but no, the aliens' ancestors usually weren't refugees. A few got here by accident, but most were exiles. Criminals."

Oh hell. "What did they do?"

"The short answer? The tol were sent to nowhere because they wouldn't fight. The chup were sent because they would."

And everyone else did what they were told, and the chup did the telling because they were willing to back up everything they said with force: the fundamental basis for the concept of government. "This station isn't being kept clean, and the procedure for dealing with the rescued is whacked. I don't think the chup are doing a very good job of running things. It might not be a bad idea to alter the situation."

Marjorie was conspicuously startled. "Well, that's different," she said. "Usually it takes weeks to get someone around to the idea of the Resistance. You're the first rescue I've even heard of who brought it up on your own. Of course, you *are* Samuel Watt."

He was pretty sure he didn't want to know what kind of myths had grown up about him. And he was pretty sure he was going to learn anyway.

He was also pretty sure the Resistance was going to turn out to have been spinning its wheels for a long time. Even assuming they somehow had any of the weapons, using them inside a space habitat certainly qualified as a defining symptom of insanity.

It occurred to him suddenly that since he was the first sent out, people weren't showing up in anything like chronological order.

It also occurred to him that the reason he was here was that Earth's transfer booths hadn't been working. "How did people get themselves sent out when the Sun was going giant?" he said.

"They did it before the expansion," she said, surprised.

"But I thought I was the first."

"Yes? Oh, you didn't get sent out during the *final* expansion! The pulse you got caught by was the last-but-one. That was how people figured out what was going on, when the neutrino count went up. In your time the Sun had been contracting for at least a thousand years, until the core got hot and dense enough to use carbon as a fusion catalyst again. Helium ignition didn't happen until the next pulse, in 2838. Everyone who was going to leave was gone by then."

"Is there *any* relationship between when people got sent and when they arrived?"

She waggled a hand. "Vaguely. The people who had themselves sent to nowhere when the transmitter was aimed through the Sun started showing up over a thousand years ago. Most people tried to go to colony worlds, but there wasn't much room for them."

"So—" There couldn't have been room here yet, could there? "Did they get sent to nowhere too?"

"Well, some must have, because they've been showing up here. We can't communicate with the colonies, so there's no way to know how many there have been. A lot, though. They arrive in random amounts. Sometimes none show up for months. Sometimes there have been so many there was no choice but to send them again immediately. Millions, just about filled the tube."

"Why can't we talk to the colonies?"

"Ask the chup, but don't expect an answer. They're in control, and they don't share information unnecessarily."

"So the tube is idle a lot of the time," he mused, wondering if there was something useful about that.

She shook her head. "The tube is never idle. We get garbage all the time, and I do mean continuously. There's radar and like that in the tubes, so the crew can spot things like people, and your survival pod. Those get pulled out fast. The rest goes into the sorting dump, in case something was missed—or someone—and then into the main habitat. A lot gets sent to Titan after that."

"How big *is* this place?" he wondered.

"Not big enough," she grumbled. "Everybody thought Titan would be ready by the time the refugees showed up, but they got here earlier than anyone thought."

In response to what he deemed an accusing frown, Sam said, "Ten thousand years was the bottom limit. And it was really back-of-the-envelope. No data at *all*. Titan, huh?"

"It gets about as much light as Earth used to. More orange, I'm told."

"What about Saturn's magnetic field?"

"What about it?"

"Uh, radiation?"

She looked surprised. "I never heard of any. It might have blown away, like Jupiter's tail is doing."

"Jupiter has a tail?"

"Not as much since I was born. It comes and goes. The last time a moon dropped in it got really thick for a while. Is it important? I can show you the pictures from the last Trojan expedition."

Sam shook his head, trying to clear it. "No. Maybe you should show me around."

"*Again*? Oh. Right. I'll just put you into a newcomer outfit and get you a list of jargon that's changed meaning, and we'll go."

The outfit was shirt, shorts, and a bag with a capacity of about a peck, all cotton (probably not, but near as) and all a bright, cheerful blue.

Sam's coloring had always looked sort of walking-dead when set against blue. It had admittedly been a great convenience for Trick-or-Treating, but the rest of the time it was a pain. "Why blue?" he said.

"To show you need things explained," Marjorie said. "Ancient usage, origin unknown but generally assumed to be from the Doppler effect. You're catching up. Red is for the people you're trying to catch up with."

The wheel he'd been on was the third one built around the receiver tube. Only one receiver had been built after all, with vacuum-tube circuitry, since that could be adjusted to accept standard transmissions as well, and there was a certain element of haste at the time. There were now thirty-eight rings around the tube.

They took a booth to the end of the tube.

There were two hundred and ninety-two rings past its end, and another under construction. These rings were larger in radius, and a great deal broader. Ramps and elevators connected the ledge of Wheel 38 to the ground of Wheel 39.

And the correct word was indisputably ground. Crops were growing. He even saw what he thought might be cows.

"My god," Sam said, looking up from the cropland to a wall that must have been half a mile away. "And there are two hundred and ninety-two more of these?"

"Two-ninety-three next year."

"You should have inflated an asteroid."

"They bleb out and pop. They're not homogeneous enough. The second try was what convinced everyone. Killed some people. Come on." She led him to an elevator—he was going to be some little while getting used to elevators with curved shafts—and said, "Garbage goes out to Wheel 330. We'll deadhead and meet some people there."

"You keep the walls in case of blowouts, right?"

Other people were waiting for the elevator, and half of them—the ones dressed scandalously and in red—stared at him until they noticed how he was dressed. Then they stared at Marjorie.

"Never been an air leak in a finished Wheel," she said. "And check your list."

Sam had a feeling he didn't have to. "Why not remove the walls?"

"It's where people live. More every day. We need the land to grow food, Sam. In multiple layers. This place is so big we're getting gravity effects at the ends, and it's still too crowded."

For the first time Sam realized that the expected arrivals had to number in the billions. "My God, how thick are the walls?"

"Five miles each."

"What are they *made* of?"

"Steel reinforced with diamond fibers, mostly. And living spaces, of course, the bottom thousand levels anyway. We've got thousands of people to a square mile here."

Times a thousand levels and hundreds of rings. "And every apartment has its own garden," he said, not asking.

"Oh yes. There are stories from back when sewage and garbage were processed biologically instead of industrially. Huge suicide and murder rates. The brain appears to be hardwired to respond to trace components of those smells with despair, sometimes leading to random fury. Current theory says it may be a survival trait to limit overcrowding. Can't have that in an environment that requires constant maintenance, so now it's all reduced and remade and separated for whatever."

He could picture the processes needed to accomplish that. She had an astonishing gift for summary; he would have felt compelled to at least mention pressure tanks, or fractional distillation, or magnets, or anyway something. Then he realized he was overcomplicating things: when reduced organics were burned you got stuff good for use by plant life, and the rest was a mixture of high-grade ore whose every ingredient was something somebody had already found useful. It wouldn't even have to be melted down, just electrolyzed in iridium tanks. (If they didn't have a lot more iridium than they needed, this whole situation was an unnecessarily elaborate hoax.)

Sam had idly come up with a rudimentary design by the time the elevator arrived, and came out of his reverie to realize that once they reached the top they were going to be riding in what was, essentially, a garbage truck. "Why isn't there a transfer booth system for this?" he said.

"There is. This is marginally cheaper for garbage, and more popular with people who like the view," said Marjorie.

"How can it be che—" he began, then thought of angular momentum. The garbage already represented a power loss: it wasn't transmitted turning. Once it got where it was wanted, paired loads could be sent from axis to rim, each used as compensator mass for the other, but teleporting it from here to there would either be insanely finicky, or screw with angular momentum. Just sending people must have been some trouble. Also, at the axis transceivers sending it to the rim, it would help a lot in measuring those masses if the junk was already in a container. "The cans are made of garbage?" he said.

"Yes, remade concrete. Saves sending them back to this end."

The elevator was big, and had seats and entertainment screens. And that damn black mildew wherever surfaces came together. "What the hell is this stuff, anyway?" he said, pointing at some.

Marjorie shook her head. "Something that came in with the first load of garbage, as far as anybody knows. It's adapted to high-tech environments, uses light and electricity and electronics waste to grow. Actually pays for its keep, it reinforces whatever it's stuck to. You have to wonder how much time the civilization it came from spent killing off its ancestors for this version to have evolved. If you want to clean it off completely you have to use fluorine or heated ozone."

It made a border around the plates of fixtures and power sockets. "How much electricity does it use?" Sam said.

"Neighborhood of one part per million, unless there's a spike. Then it eats the surplus and stores it, or sends it along to a neighbor."

"It sounds like someone invented it as a living surge protector."

"That's one theory. Others have suggested an ancestor was designed as a weapon to bring down an enemy's infrastructure, but all the other strains worked too fast to spread far."

Like Ebola couldn't, before transfer booths. "So it started as a wolf, and what you've got now is a collie?"

Marjorie flinched. "Don't mention dogs around me, okay? A long time back people were breeding them to attack the chup, and there were a lot of deaths. Orientation requires studying everything."

Sam nodded. Get back on topic. "So the chup and the tol don't know where it came from either."

"Not a clue."

Sam considered. "First load, huh? None since then?"

"Not that I've heard."

And she would have. "It sounds to me like somebody made the stuff as it is, and somebody else panicked and threw it away immediately. Otherwise there ought to be more than one type. Anybody ever succeed in giving it a close examination?"

Marjorie tilted her head and looked at him interestedly. "At least some of your reputation must be based on fact," she said. "It is *incredibly* difficult to examine. Light is soaked up, and a scanning electron microscope tears it apart. The individual components are no more than virus-sized, but seem to be much more complex on the inside."

"Well, yeah," he said, surprised that she sounded surprised. "A virus is no more than a parasite. These things apparently operate without a host. What's the light converter, gold leaf over selenium? I *know* it's not silicon." In atmosphere, one of those wore out before it could generate enough power to make another.

She shook her head. "The surface has a thin layer of iridium, and its texture is chaotically pitted. Funnels light inside and keeps it there. Whatever converts light to power is internal."

Sam touched the patch he'd pointed at. It was no warmer than the metal near it. "Does a damn good job, too," he said.

"Oh?"

"No waste heat. Not even from conducting the power to areas that aren't close to a socket. And those wires have to be *thin*. Superconductor?"

Marjorie opened her mouth, furrowed her brow, and said, "I don't think so. People would be stripping it off everything." She touched a window, and it turned out to be a screen. She typed rapidly on the bottom half for a while, then said, "Those are silicon. Not the metallic form; chemically bonded together, and held in place by linked organic side chains. The electron clouds of silicon atoms blur together, so a charge applied to one can be drawn off any connected silicon atom."

"And the side chains insulate the silicon from air. I remember that about silicon. Not exactly superconduction, more like static. Nobody ever got it to work on a large scale, it reverts to the crystal state. This lifeform sounds like the only application."

"There's nanomachinery," she said.

"Life *is* nanomachinery. What worries me now is what happened to whoever made this stuff." He felt himself getting lighter. "We're slowing down."

"Almost there. Need a bag for low gravity?"

"No, I'm lucky that way."

"Okay." She shut off the screen, and the window view reappeared. Then it disappeared again, as they entered the hub.

Her question drew his attention to his stomach. "Where's the nearest place to get something to eat?" he said. "Just cell fuel isn't going to make it."

"How long since you ate last?—I do not believe I just said that," she said, as all the other guides grinned at her. She looked unhappy.

Sam sympathized with her. "About fifteen subjective hours," he said. "I could really go for some popcorn," he added, in a deliberate attempt to divert everyone's minds.

He was successful beyond his wildest dreams. Every one of the guides glared at him, and one said, "You creep."

"Uh," Sam said.

"There's no maize here," said Marjorie. "The chup won't allow it."

"Allergies?"

"Cheapskates. Turns out it causes all kinds of medical problems. The worst are probably kidney stones and compulsive eating."

Sam shook his head violently. "Are we talking about the same thing?"

The guide who'd called him a creep said, "Giant grain glomerule, one to three hands long, seeds usually yellow, unusually juicy for a grain. Sorry I was rude. From your expression you feel just the way I do about it. Joseph Abagnale, Junior. Call me Jayjay." He was a big husky guy with blond hair and skin about the shade of Sam's. He stuck out his hand.

Sam took it. "Sam Watt." He knew that name, but he was so jazzed up he couldn't place it at first.

Jayjay held very still and studied him from head to foot with lightning speed. "I will be goddamned," he said. "You really are—I was the first person after you to take the Long Jump."

He was clearly one of those people who can pronounce capitals, and that made the difference. Sam snapped his fingers and pointed at him. "You were the Technologist candidate for President! I voted for you," he said.

"That was you?" said Jayjay, smiling faintly.

Sam nodded, scowled, and made a few abortive gestures in an attempt to express his exasperation. "People don't *listen*," he finally got out.

"Hence my departure. You know, a certain amount of co-incidence crops up all the time here, but I like this one." He studied Sam's face for a moment, then added, "You're capable of killing someone. I strongly urge you to avoid the Resistance. They have an awful lot of argumentative people with no sensible plan, and I came close to killing one guy myself."

"I don't think I'd kill anybody," Sam said, shocked.

Jayjay shrugged. "Hold that thought. I've been wrong about people occasionally. But if I had a crack at getting some popcorn, I wouldn't want to be held accountable for what I'd do."

"How long have you been here?" Sam said.

"Be ninety years in September," said Jayjay. When Sam goggled at him, he grinned and said, "If you think you feel better now, just wait three weeks. Genetic reboot has some amazing effects."

"He's already manifested some," said Marjorie, and guides and newbies alike all grinned. "More than usual so soon," she added, and the guides all looked at Sam.

"Hey, how about those Knicks?" said Sam.

The only one who laughed was Jayjay, but since the rest looked baffled Sam counted it as a success.

Then he was distracted. They had gotten through the barrier, which had been the original hull of the station, and were in the hub itself.

Everybody got out of the elevator.

After a few seconds, Jayjay said, "Now, while they're looking up, we quickly steal all their stuff." Sam ignored him. A few seconds later, Jayjay said, "He's the real thing."

"I know," said Marjorie.

That got Sam's attention, and he looked at them by turns. "What?"

"You're the only one who kept looking up," said Jayjay. "What do you think?"

"I think Marjorie finds it crowded because her ancestors had the place to themselves for so long," Sam said, looking up again.

There was just enough gravity to notice, and judging by what he took to be man-width curved ramps coming down, the core shaft was at least five hundred yards above them. It took up a third of the field of view, more or less, which made it about that big across, and it had faint noises coming from it.

"Industry?" he said.

"Sure. People who kept doing industry on Earth after space travel must have been crazy," Marjorie told him. "Lots easier in microgravity. And safer."

"Bit of a commute before JumpShift, but I see your point," Sam said. There were fine details on the shaft, which he took to be pipes and cables and … the supports for the conveyor system. Partway around the curve of the deck, he saw an oblong polished gray object come out of the wall from the direction of the receiver tube. He'd seen pictures of oil tankers. It looked about that big.

He was not at all sanguine about seeing it fitting itself into a collection of looped cables. Evidently they were not going to be traveling inside the core.

"Has there ever been a cable failure?" he said.

"Never," said Marjorie. "But if you'll look at the hull, you'll see—"

"It's self-transmitting! Where does it take us?"

"It doesn't. There are booths on top, and when a falling car is empty it goes straight to a drop cage around Titan. At least, it will if there's ever a tube failure. Oh my God, did you think it hung from the cables the whole trip?" She grew wide-eyed, but managed to keep from actually laughing.

There was one other European-pink newcomer, a very old one: he was next to bald, had thick glasses on and some kind of powered exoskeleton around the lower half of his body, and his skin had more age spots than spaces between them. He had been working his way over to them for a couple of minutes, and now said, "You didn't notice some of the details up there are refracting light?" He pointed. "Clear tubes."

"I'm kind of nearsighted."

"And you were going anyway? You must have about six balls. Theodore Kyle." He held out a hand to shake.

"Sam Watt."

"Recognized you." Theodore's voice dropped for a moment. "Work it, kid—so this place started out as your idea?" he added in normal volume. "Thanks. Saved the human race, in which I take a proprietary interest." There was nothing wrong with his upper-body strength; his handshake encased without compression, as if he were holding a small frightened animal to keep it from falling. Theodore showed some of the wasting of extreme age, but Sam had the distinct impression that Theodore could have tossed him over his shoulder onto a hatrack.

"You know, you seem familiar too," Sam said.

"Nah, I'm just sociable—I'm kidding." In a rasping voice Theodore said, "'*Spyin' on me with rays, I* tole *'em, millennium hand and shrimp!*'" As Sam's jaw dropped with recognition, Theodore grinned and added, "I had a long career doing voice work for animation, until the KS stopped helping. Took off rather than spend all my money on a funeral and inheritance taxes. Turns out you *can* take it with you." He got out a perfectly-normal-looking credit card. "I even have some left after paying for my rescue and medical bills."

Sam was jolted. Of course there'd be bills. But nobody was nagging yet—"What in the world did you bring that they can't make here?"

"Mint copies of every comic book scripted by Alfred Bester."

Sam just gaped. He was in the presence of Genius. Of course someone would have thought of all the famous big-name comics; there were probably multiple sets of the complete run of, say, Batman. Then he said, "How did you transport them?"

"In the back of a Marsbuggy. Got a nice piece of change for it, too. Vintage and all that. I had to assume the receiver wouldn't have air in it, so I took everything I wanted in one go. How's your heart?"

"Still under warranty when I left."

"Oh, you had one grown? Good, that'll help when you get the bill."

"What's the economic setup?" Sam said.

"Radical," said Theodore with great gravity. "Arbitrary tokens of symbolic value are awarded to you, based on the benefit you've provided to everyone else in the world put together, in their collective opinion of its value. It's called *money*."

Sam blinked, snorted, and was starting to laugh when another newcomer came forward and said, "That's not how money actually works."

"It's not how it's *treated*," Theodore said over his shoulder, "but it is *precisely* what it actually *is*."

The man behind him smiled smugly and said, "I'm an economist."

He was going to say more, but Theodore had turned and knocked him out. The man was still in the air, receding, as Theodore turned back and said, "I owe Clint Eastwood's estate a penny. One of his movies included the fact that if you hit someone hard enough to turn his head all the way to the side, there's an off switch. Saddest story I ever saw. Wouldn't have missed it, though. Your credit's definitely good here, in case you're worried."

The economist's guide had run after her charge, and while fetching him back called out, "What the hell did you hit him for?"

Theodore turned. "I grew up during the Seventy Years' War. I *know* what happens to a society where people listen to economists. You keep him quiet, I've had experience whipping up an angry mob."

"We should head for the transport," said Marjorie, in an inspired diversion.

They did that. On the way, Theodore stayed by Sam, having apparently adopted him. Sam didn't mind, since it made him The Kid, which was a change he liked. "That was a hell of a punch," Sam said.

"I'm horribly strong," Theodore said. "Spent over a century holding myself up with canes before the folks here gave me the walker." He rapped the exoskeleton, then held out his hands. Their relaxed state was curled. "It's a loaner. I'll be able to give it back in about two weeks. Already been here a week, getting fitted. I *like* this place."

"Me too," said Sam. "Don't know what an obsolete engineer is going to do to pay the bills, though." He was remembering what his new heart had cost. It had cleaned out most of his assets. (Socialized medicine would have been much cheaper; without the profit motive for medical researchers, all he'd have needed was a funeral.)

"Need a loan?"

Sam recalled something from Mark Twain. "I'd rather have the friend than the money," he said. "Something will turn up. After all, I did."

"Fair enough. You were sent by mistake? You still look kind of worn, so I'd guess you're fresh out of the box. No convalescence."

"Yeah."

And it all came crashing in on him. Sam stopped walking, felt the stinging inside his nose, and found himself fighting not to cry. If not for the negligible gravity he'd have folded up on the deck.

Theodore said, "Yup, new," put Sam over his shoulder, and kept walking.

"I'll be okay," Sam said. "I'll get over it."

"Good," said Theodore, and kept walking without putting Sam down.

"I just need something to eat."

"That's right, you haven't had anything in a hundred and sixty-one centuries," Theodore said.

And he leaned forward.

Later, Sam was never quite able to piece together the events of the next minute or so to his own satisfaction. The contributing elements were the fact of being carried by someone who liked him, low gravity, a floor that curved upward, and leg braces that Sam later learned had been adapted from a spacesuit designed for emergency work under high thrust. Sam recalled moving very fast, occasionally getting quite far from the deck, and a new (and receding) female voice shouting, "Theodore, stop that, you're top-heavy!"

Sam found himself set neatly on the deck, not far from another elevator, as Theodore flipped completely over him. He turned in time to see Theodore doing a couple more flips as he came to a stop, using them to lose momentum. Theodore bounded back in one go, grinned, and said, "One of the things that made me really popular with the studios was I learn *fast*. I've been practicing with these all week."

"Not all week," said a chubby Oriental woman in red coveralls as she caught up. "God dammit, you loon, you're worse than a kitten. Don't give me the eyes!" she added as Theodore turned to her.

Theodore picked her up and kissed her.

The rest of the crowd had caught up by the time he put her back down. "No fair," she said, looking and sounding dazed.

"You never said a word about the tongue," Theodore said.

"Shut up," she said, without any great conviction.

"Sam, this is Natalya Vasquez. She's my keeper. The chup may be mommies from hell, but they are bloody astounding matchmakers. They're the ones who choose who a newcomer gets for orientation. Which is damned generous when you consider they don't approve of the procedure. Any chup you'd want to talk with is female. They run everything. The males are bigger and may tactfully be described as thick, and are pretty much kept around for reproduction and heavy lifting."

"Oh. Just like us, then."

Theodore laughed, nodded, and said, "Only more so."

Another group was approaching the elevator from the other direction, and it included a chup. This one was wearing white, and there was something in her movements that made her seem less instantly confrontational than Davoost.

Still armed and armored, though. She was holding something like a thick phone in one hand, studying the screen, and appeared to be chewing with her mouth open. Sam had begun wondering if that signified annoyance when he became distracted by the approach of an oversized camper. It looked like the kind people used to build from discarded freight cars.

As he stared, a speaker on the front said, "You guys want a ride?"

Everybody in the group with the chup looked at the chup. She swallowed air and said, "Go ahead," and almost everybody moved over to their left. Three headed for the other side; Sam reckoned that two were Japanese, and the third must be from Canada or the UK. The main camper door was on the driver's right, though.

"People with kids go in the back section," said the driver, who then saw that nobody had any along. "Okay, people who don't mind kids go in the back section." With everyone aboard, the camper's forward population went from about ten to about thirty, with only one pair going through the door into the back. Sounded like a party in there. The chup with them sat quietly in a corner. There were still plenty of unoccupied seats. The driver just drove straight onto the elevator, which took them up to the deck of the barge.

The people in the front, at least, were mostly Caucasian. It made sense if they all knew each other.

Some of the people in the camper were playing a fantasy wargame, though they at least looked like grownups. (Sam, who at eleven had designed a diode tube that required neither a heated filament nor beta-emitter cathode doping, had never seen the attraction of roleplaying games. Reality had his full attention.) A plush and portly round-headed calico cat (black, brown, and fawn) was walking around on the table and hitting players up for contributions.

Sam was still feeling rocky and had never seen a calico cat in those colors, so he went over to have a look at her. She came up to him, inspected his hand when offered, and stood on her back legs to prop herself up and inspect his face. He picked her up, and the players all went quiet and looked at them. "What?" he said.

"Chocolate Chip never lets anyone pick her up," said the only one with multiple screens, presumably the ref. He spoke without emphasis and showed no expression, and Sam got the impression he was waiting for something extreme to happen.

What happened was, the cat hit Sam in the chin with her head.

As one, the players exhaled and went back to what they were doing.

Sam sat in a nearby seat and began scratching places that were difficult to reach. He noticed a little of the conversation: "Okay, we can pick any champion with a well-known literary source?"

"Yes, except Achilles, he's on the other side."

"*You*—Fine. Parley."

"About what?"

"We want to try settling this without a battle." Pause. "Our negotiator is Jacob Marley."

"… You bastard."

As the referee began expostulating about the amount of work he'd done, Marjorie sat by Sam, and Chocolate Chip gave her a blink before resuming her attention to him. "Is that a Masius?" Marjorie said.

"I don't know from breeds," said Sam. The camper moved onto the top of the barge, and Sam said, "Do they put, like, a mobile restaurant on a barge?"

"No, just food dispensers. You type in your order and somebody fixes it and sends it to you." Marjorie looked past him and said, "Like that one—how did you guys afford this?" she said, pointing at what looked like a teller machine with a glandular condition. (And that metal mildew at the joins.)

A very black woman who wasn't playing called across the camper, "We brought a poster done by an art student in the style of Toulouse-Lautrec." She was smiling. Had a trace of one of those nifty Central African accents that were already rare in Sam's time.

"Waiwaiwait," said Theodore. "*Ladies at the Café?*"

"You know it?"

"I met the guy who appraised it. My God, you must be rich."

"Actually we're art thieves. It was locked up in a *warehouse*," she said indignantly.

"I meant now."

"Oh. Yeah," she agreed. "Other stuff let us build the Big Bus here for our families, but we kept that one. Kind of the gem of the collection."

"I never heard of it," Sam said.

"The struggling young artist was Pablo Picasso," Theodore said, and went over to sit by the woman. Natalya sat with them. There was a tiny blonde woman in red seated next to the woman who was already there.

They began conversing in low voices. After a minute the black woman said, "Holy crap! Engineer Watt, order anything you want."

Sam began the process of setting Chocolate Chip aside, and one claw poked into his hand, with the strong suggestion of nine, no, eleven more available if needed. "Marjorie, I appear to be trapped. Would you get me a ham sandwich?"

"Sam, there's fusion power here," she said. "Recycling and supercropping to feed fifty billion people. There's anything to eat you could want."

Sam nodded. "Good. I want a ham sandwich."

Shaking her head, she got up and went to the food dispenser.

"And another slice of ham on the side," Sam said. Chocolate Chip began kneading his lap.

That was a smart cat. The windows here obviously weren't connected to the station system, so Sam looked in the bag Marjorie had given him, and yes, there was a screen in it. He looked up "Masius"—he had plenty of experience using a screen with one hand—and found that they were named for a 21st-century philanthropist who had begun collecting cats with functional extra digits. The round heads held bigger brains; the reference page had links to stories of them rescuing their humans by knocking them out of the way of danger, setting off alarms, and tearing the throats out of armed attackers—all of which he had heard of other cats doing, but there were also cases of them using the emergency speed dial and arranging deadfall traps, which was a bit out of the usual league.

"*The Boy Who Drew Cats*," Sam recalled. "You're a temple cat, aren't you?" he said, scratching her cheek, and she washed his hand a little before reaching up and pulling it to the other side of her face.

On a hunch he looked up rats. They were listed as an extinct pest.

He just bet they were.

As the carrier got fitted into the tube and began moving, Marjorie returned with what would have been an amazingly good sandwich even if he weren't ravenous. Chocolate Chip accepted offerings of ham—which Marjorie had foresightedly had cut into strips—with dignified approval, lifting her head and opening her mouth after each piece was gone. He'd halfway expected her to pick up the pieces and put them into her mouth (which he had seen another extra-toe cat do with peas), but this was apparently the job of her staff, i.e., Sam.

Marjorie had seen he was busy, and was dozing. That seemed like a plan, but he decided to do some browsing to learn about the station.

This proved difficult. The screen connected up fine, but an argument had started at the table: "Every ruler isn't Lawful!"

"Effective rulers are," said the guy who'd picked Marley.

"What about Ming the Merciless? He never keeps his word!"

"Then you admit he's consistent."

Sam nudged Marjorie, picked up Chocolate Chip, and moved up to join the group sitting close to the driver. There was still noise—("Lincoln was Lawful! He imposed conscription and income tax." "Both unconstitutional, and he also freed the slaves without paying for them. Chaotic.")—but it wasn't too bad here.

Another chup came out of the back section and spoke to the one who had stayed: "I need you as a witness, this one's got a jammer too. Mocking a child."

"I was making a joke!" said the woman she had in tow.

"Conversation," said the chup. "'Hey Mom, you know there's no word that rhymes with radio either?' Reply: 'Desconsadio.' Four hundred hours unpaid labor in ninety days."

"Open and shut," said the other chup, and took the woman's picture.

"So you're the law?" the woman said.

"No, you people make the laws. We just enforce them. Some we enjoy more than others," said her escort, and took her into the back again.

Chocolate Chip had to nudge Sam's hand to get him scratching again. "Marjorie," he said, "I'm not sure I want to join the Resistance after all."

A big beige man in a red three-piece suit looked at Sam and said, "You euphemism."

Chocolate Chip got off Sam's lap without prompting when his legs stiffened up, and Sam lunged across the aisle and punched the man at the left corner of his jaw. Then he tried to curl his entire body around his hand, which hurt amazingly.

The chup stopped Sam's bouncing around the room from recoil, and pushed him into his seat. By then what was left of his headache pill had kicked in, and his hand just felt big and fragile. He looked at the guide he'd punched. That man was *out*. Other guides were giving him first aid. "Son of a bitch, it works," Sam said.

"What was that about?" said the chup.

Despite her aggressive voice, Sam didn't feel threatened. "He called me … a name whose meaning I deduced from tone and context. Is this a professional question?"

"Yes."

"He called me a 'euphemism.'"

After the barest perceptible pause, and with no change of tone or stance, the chup said, "Are you going to hit him again?"

"Not unless I find out it's even worse than I thought," Sam said.

"Very well," said the chup. "I do not intend to get him fired for that, as you are not his charge." She went back to her seat.

Marjorie, who had been staring at Sam in considerable wonder, said, "That was very perceptive. Let me see your hand." She found no broken bones, but his wrist was swelling up, and she wrapped it and gave him a different pill. "It's not a painkiller," she said when he told her the last one was still working. "It's noradrenalin."

The stuff they shot berserks with. Fair enough, he was getting hot.

Chocolate Chip got back on his lap, and he began checking out the station specs.

It produced enough internal heat that the outside was painted black to radiate it away. (It was a good idea, but Sam couldn't find out who'd thought it up. Pity.) Theresa had apparently been right about the tol power system … no, she hadn't, because the lithium-proton power stations in each ring were labeled "Joule-Philips" plants. He checked, and the tol used cesium-fluorine one-shot cells. Their suit carried several in case of mistransmission—every one a potential bomb.

"The tol must have the sheer guts of a kitten," he muttered.

"They're parasites," said Marjorie. "On Thlook—I can't say that quite right—anyway, at home their hosts are enormous herd animals. I can't say that one at all, I'm afraid."

It made sense. Sam vaguely recalled reading a point someone had made about courage and the flea.

He indulged his morbid curiosity by checking the cost of rescue and repair. It normally came to three million Q and change. One Q was a kilowatt-hour of 110 volt 60 hertz electricity. Sam liked the idea of money having real value, and idly wondered if Theodore's knuckles hurt.

Sam decided to check his own balance, and the screen asked him for his password. Not an ID, just a password. Interesting. The heart of the system must have come from the *Norman Dean*. He typed in *gulag101* and let the screen take his picture for biometrics.

For a moment the screen displayed two columns, of words and numerals, most of the numbers having at least eight or nine figures; the only thing he caught from the word column was "JumpShift Shares," with a very large number opposite that. Then the screen lit up with:

COMPLEMENT COMPLETE.

ALL STAND BY FOR TRANSMISSION.

There were outcries from the gamers, mostly on the theme of "Transmission of what?" He felt the transport system stop moving. The faint sounds that had been coming from overhead stopped too.

Then, for just an instant, he was agonizingly cold.

Then he was warm again, but shaking with reaction to the chill. That is, the physical chill. The one he was feeling now was mental.

Dreading the result, he looked out the camper window. The cropland of the ring they were passing through was still visible, though.

Abruptly, his screen, along with everybody else's, announced in a warm, reassuring voice:

"This is the Samuel Watt Rescue Station Extended Maintenance System. We have confirmed that the station owner has arrived, and have therefore completed our mission by bringing it back to our home system. There will be delays in some services for up to two days, as all reserve supplies of materials and food were transported to the Titan project and its supply ships prior to departure. This was why all nonsupport systems have been powered down. They may be restarted at your convenience. Fresh resources are available for replenishment here. If anyone has any questions, an induction device can be used to open communication with any part of the Extended Maintenance System. It looks like this."

And the screen displayed that damn metal mildew.

"Thank you for your patience, and welcome to our home."

And his screen again displayed a significant fraction of the wealth of the human race, in Sam's name.

The idea of establishing a station to collect aliens and their knowledge had been a good one, but somebody else had had it first, and better: send out self-replicators to alien receivers, have them form a complete shell around whatever they found (Black paint? Black paint!), infiltrate the controls of everything, and *take the whole shebang home.*

"Well. God. Damn. It," Sam said. "There weren't three intelligent species aboard. There were four."

Chocolate Chip hove a great sigh, stood in his lap, looked up at him, and said, "Five."

THE STELLAR GUILD BOOKS

Tau Ceti
by Kevin J. Anderson & Steven Savile

Reboots
by Mercedes Lackey & Cody Martin

On The Train
by Harry & Rachel Turtledove

When the Blue Shift Comes
by Robert Silverberg & Alvaro Zinos-Amaro

New Under the Sun
by Nancy Kress & Therese Pieczynski

The Aethers of Mars
by Eric Flint & Charles E. Gannon

Red Tide
by Larry Niven, Brad R. Torgersen & Matthew J. Harrington

9 781612 421322